THE
GHOSTS
OF
SKELETON
CANYON

THE GHOSTS OF SKELETON CANYON

A NOVEL BY

ROBERT W. CALLIS

iUniverse

THE GHOSTS OF SKELETON CANYON

iUniverse books may be ordered through booksellers or by contacting:

iUniverse
1663 Liberty Drive
Bloomington, IN 47403
www.iuniverse.com
1-800-Authors (1-800-288-4677)

Because of the dynamic nature of the Internet, any web addresses or links contained in this book may have changed since publication and may no longer be valid. The views expressed in this work are solely those of the author and do not necessarily reflect the views of the publisher, and the publisher hereby disclaims any responsibility for them.

Any people depicted in stock imagery provided by Thinkstock are models, and such images are being used for illustrative purposes only. Certain stock imagery © Thinkstock.

ISBN: 978-1-4917-6588-3 (sc)
ISBN: 978-1-4917-6589-0 (e)

Library of Congress Control Number: 2015905898

Print information available on the last page.

iUniverse rev. date: 04/10/2015

DEDICATION

To Ed and Laurel Snyder, my friends and college classmates at Iowa Wesleyan College. Ed and Laurel reside in Tucson, Arizona, and have been great hosts and guides during my visits to Arizona to research this story.

PROLOGUE

East of St. Louis, Missouri
September 11, 1886

Massai awoke from his sleeping position on the hard wooden floor of the white man's train car. He could feel the vibrations of the train's wheels running on the steel tracks as they shuddered through the floorboards of the car. The air was hot and dusty. His throat felt dry and his lacerated, blood encrusted fingertips hurt from his previous efforts. There was little ventilation and the smell of urine and human feces was a jolt to his senses. It was the morning of the fourth day since the white soldiers had roughly loaded Massai and the other Apaches onto the train cars at Ft. Bowie. Many of the soldiers had taken advantage of the situation to land an angry blow to the defenseless Apaches as the Indians boarded the train.

A careful look around the train car showed many of his fellow Chiricahua Apaches were still asleep. Massai again felt the rage in his chest that he knew he must control. He was filled with anger against the treachery of the white soldiers and the stupidity of Geronimo and his followers.

Before Geronimo had surrendered, the white soldiers had sent all of the remaining Chiricahua Apache men, women, and children on a train like this one to some place called Florida. After the white soldiers had captured Geronimo and his band, they were not only sending them to Florida, but the soldiers also included all of the remaining Chiricahua Apaches, including the sixty who had served as loyal army scouts, helping the soldiers track down the renegade Apaches. The scouts reward was to be treated like criminals. Massai had served as an army scout, and he was among the sixty.

Since the first day Massai had positioned himself next to one of the train car windows. He did this by forcing other Apaches out of his way until he got what he wanted. Massai was a large man for an Apache. He was almost six feet tall and broad at the shoulders. He was lean with ropey muscles and very strong. He was well known among the Apache for his endurance. He had spent years training under his father in the desert and mountains, learning his woodcraft until he could move about as though he was invisible.

Massai took his place next to the window and pretended to be looking out at the scenery. He rubbed the torn skin on his fingertips to get the dried blood off of them. In fact, he was taking the last three nails out of the window that locked it to the wooden frame. When he first sat by the window, he could see the window had been nailed shut. For three days he had been slowly and carefully removing the nails and then replacing them back in their holes where he could easily remove them, but to a casual observer, the window was still nailed securely closed.

Within an hour, he had the remaining three nails pulled out. Now he sat and waited. After almost two more hours had passed, he could feel the train car under him was slowing down, and he could see the terrain outside his window also slowing down.

Carefully he looked around the train car. No one in the train car was paying any attention to him. As luck would have it, the two white soldiers who were guarding the Apaches had left the car to get some coffee, pausing only to kick a sleeping Apache who they decided was in their way.

Massai looked out the window and could see the reason the train was slowing down was because they had begun to go up a steep grade. He had learned earlier that the train would have to slow down when it went up hills.

He knew instinctively this was his chance. He quickly stood, pulled hard at the window until it gave way to his pressure and slid up and open. Then he leaned out the window on his back and reached up until he found a handhold on the outside window frame. Using his strong arms he pulled himself through the window. Then he used his legs to kick himself away from the train car and found himself falling. He tucked his body into a ball and hit the ground hard. Small sharp rocks dug into his body as he rolled down an embankment before finally coming to a stop at the bottom of a dry wash.

Massai picked himself up and found, except for a few cuts and bruises, he was not hurt. He looked to the east and could see the smoke from the train still heading east. None of the white soldiers had seen him leap from the train. He turned and faced the west and began walking along the railroad tracks of the white man's train.

One year and twelve hundred miles later, Massai had returned to his Chiricahua Apache homeland in Arizona. During his journey, no one, not Indian or white man, ever saw a sign of him. Massai was home, and he was determined to make the white man and his fellow Apache pay for their treachery.

CHAPTER ONE

PRESENT DAY

KIT TOSSED HIS OVERNIGHT BAG in the back of the cab of his white Ford F-150 pickup truck and looked at his watch. It was 5:10. He was meeting Swifty for breakfast at the Café Ritz in Kemmerer at 5:30. He paused to take in a deep breath of the cold, crisp early morning air. Wyoming mornings were cold, even in the summer.

Fifteen minutes later he pulled up in front of the café and walked in the front door expecting Swifty would be late. To his surprise he had seen Swifty's black Ford pick-up truck parked outside, and he saw Swifty at a corner table drinking coffee. Swifty's curly brown hair peeked out from under his cowboy hat. His mischievous brown eyes seemed unusually serious. To Kit's further amazement, Swifty was actually reading a newspaper.

Kit pulled out a chair at the table and said, "Been here long?" The café opened at 5:00 every morning to accommodate the local ranchers and also the miners either coming off or getting ready to start a shift at the coal mine.

Swifty dropped his newspaper to the side of the table, but not before Kit noticed that the paper was three days old. He was pretty sure Swifty had just found the paper and picked it up as a prop to pimp Kit.

"I been here since the damn place opened. Where the hell have you been?"

Kit smiled at his best friend. "I'm five minutes early. We agreed to meet at 5:30 this morning."

"That so? I don't seem to recall agreeing to 5:30."

"You're lucky that tiny brain of yours can remember anything. I doubt you can even remember your own birthday."

"Can so. It's September 29, every year."

"I'm in shock. Let me write this down for the benefit of historians everywhere."

Kit reached into his jacket pocket with an exaggerated motion and pulled out a small spiral notebook and a pen.

Swifty just gave him a look of distain until Kit returned the objects to his jacket pocket.

"Got your bags all packed?"

"Yep," replied Kit.

"Did you remember to pack some protection?"

"Get your mind out of the gutter. This is a first date with a girl I barely know. I'll be lucky to get a good night kiss."

"With your style, you'll be lucky to get a handshake."

The waitress arrived with a fresh cup of coffee for Kit and a refill for Swifty.

"What'll you boys have this morning?" she asked.

"I'll have the usual and make sure you give the bill to my good man here," said Swifty.

"Good man my ass," said Kit.

"I am shocked and appalled at your behavior, sir," said Swifty.

The waitress, a middle aged single mother named Sally, laughed at the exchange between the two friends. She had heard similar lines from the two cowboys many times.

"I'll have the number three," said Kit.

Sally grinned and left for the kitchen with their orders stored in her memory, as she had written nothing down on her pad.

"So what exactly is your plan for this week-end," asked Swifty?

Kit carefully took a sip of coffee before answering Swifty. Finally he set his coffee cup down and looked Swifty in the eye.

"What I got planned for this week-end and what I actually do are none of your business."

"Ahah! That means you have no plan. That should surprise no one."

Kit failed to take the bait and just sat back and took another sip of coffee.

After about two minutes of silence, Swifty twisted his lean and well-muscled body around in his chair. He couldn't stand it anymore and he blurted out, "You gotta tell me what happens. I'm your best friend."

Kit looked up from behind his coffee cup.

"Friends don't pry into what is none of their business."

"Okay, okay, I get it. I'll quit asking questions, although I am appalled at your lack of planning for one of the biggest moments of your short and uneventful life."

Kit set his coffee cup down on the table and smiled at Swifty. "Here's my plan. I'm driving to Boulder, Colorado, which will take most of today. I've reserved a room at the Boulderado Hotel in Boulder. After I check in, I'll call Shirley and set up a time for dinner. Then I'll pick her up at her apartment and take her to dinner."

"That's it! That's all you got?"

"My plan is to just take it slow and get to know each other and see what happens."

"I thought there was some kind of connection or magic moment when she took care of you up in the Wind River Mountains."

Kit paused and took a sip of his coffee before replying.

"Swifty, she's a nurse. She does stuff like this all the time. Taking her out to dinner is a thank you for what she did and hopefully more will develop."

"Boring. Really boring. How did I get stuck with such a boring, plain vanilla guy for a friend."

"Actually I noticed there is no long line of people waiting for the chance to be your friend. So maybe I'm boring and dumb as well."

Swifty started to sputter and then realized he was having his chain yanked, and he broke out in a broad grin and a deep chuckle.

"You're too deep for me, college boy. I just hope you have fun and manage to stay out of trouble. I'll keep my cell phone on in case you get tossed in jail or manage to irritate some of the locals."

"I appreciate that, Swifty, but I don't foresee anything like that happening."

"That's one of your problems. You never foresee anything until it hits you in the mouth."

"One of many of my shortcomings, I'm sure," replied Kit.

Swifty noticed a look of puzzlement on Kit's face.

"What's wrong, college boy? You look like you might be getting a case of cold feet."

"I'm not getting cold feet. It's just that I remembered that the last time I talked to Shirley on the phone she mentioned that she had something she wanted to talk to me about when I got to Boulder."

"That can't be good," said Swifty."

"We'll see. I guess I'll find out when I get to Boulder."

When they had finished breakfast and paid their bill, the two tall, lanky cowboys shook hands outside the café.

"Keep your powder dry, Kit."

"Same to you, Swifty."

Swifty stood on the sidewalk as Kit backed his pickup out of the parking spot and headed east out of town. Swifty touched his right hand to the brim of his cowboy hat in salute, quietly wishing that he was headed to Boulder with Kit.

CHAPTER TWO

KIT WAS MAKING GOOD TIME as he passed by the small hamlet of Opal in the soft light of dawn. He remembered when he and Big Dave had stopped at the old fashioned Opal Mercantile to buy parts for the stove in his sheep camp. Not long after that, he passed the small hamlet of Granger. He looked out at the weathered buildings and tried to make out the small shack that had been a Pony Express station, but there was not yet enough light.

Kit slowed down as he approached the access road to Interstate 80. He reduced his truck's speed and came to a stop on the side of the highway just opposite the site on the shoulder of the road where he had gotten stuck in the snow so long ago. It was a moment that had changed his life forever. It was there he had met Big Dave, who had stopped to rescue him from the snowbank Kit's car was buried in. Smiling to himself, Kit took his foot off the brake and pressed down on the truck's accelerator and very shortly pulled onto eastbound Interstate 80 about forty minutes after he had left the Kemmerer city limits.

Heading east on the interstate, Kit was temporarily blinded as the sun came up in his eyes as he passed Little America. He reached up and retrieved his sunglasses and put them on to deal with the sun's sudden glare. He wasn't sure how this week-end would go, but he certainly felt he owed Shirley a dinner for her help when he had been shot near the Wind River Mountains. Kit reached his arm up and rubbed the spot on his shoulder that now sported a scar from the bullet wound. He had been lucky the shotgun shell was a light load and that the pellets had not hit any bone or anything vital. He wondered what it was that Shirley wanted to talk to him about. Kit looked down at his trip odometer. Only 380 miles to Boulder he thought with a grin.

Two hours later, he found himself pulling into a truck stop to refuel just west of the city of Rawlins. He filled up the truck and hit the restroom. He bought a cup of coffee and walked out to his truck. Although the sun was up, the air was still cold. He looked to the north at the vast expanse of the Red Desert. He had passed the meager attempts by some to build homes and live on the inhospitable desert. Most of them were shacks in various states of disrepair and some were falling in on themselves. The weather-beaten boards appeared to be starving for paint as they rotted away under the relentless desert sun and the cold winds and snow of a Wyoming winter.

Driving on Interstate 80 was not a trip for sightseers. The road was on high plains desert and the landscape was dry and barren, broken only by the occasional tree or bush and the occasional hulk of an abandoned gas station. When Kit finally saw Elk Mountain in his windshield, it was a welcome relief from the dry, rocky, and treeless terrain he had been watching.

Elk Mountain was a strange place. Like the name said, it was good habitat for elk and got lots of attention from hunters during the elk season in Wyoming. It was also a historic magnet for the worst weather in Wyoming. If it was snowing in Laramie, it was a blizzard at Elk Mountain. If it was quiet in Rawlins, it was a windstorm at Elk Mountain. It almost seemed like there was a black cloud hanging over the top of the mountain that never went away.

Today there were a few clouds, but no bad weather and Kit passed by the mountain and began the slight descent into Laramie. He stopped in Laramie for a quick lunch, and he filled the truck's gas tank. Within an hour, he was entering the west end of Cheyenne. He pulled off to the side of the road and got out to walk and stretch his legs. He looked up to the north and was rewarded by the sight of eight antelope grazing along a hillside.

"I bet you don't see that on the edge of Denver," he thought. At Cheyenne, he exited Interstate 80 and headed south on Interstate 25 for Denver.

After about twenty miles, he saw the large sign on the side of the road announcing "Welcome to Colorful Colorado." This was Kit's first trip to Colorado and he could see the Rocky Mountains to his west, but only a bare outline of them was visible. He was pretty sure he was looking at the foothills that stood on the eastern edge of the Rockies.

The landscape around him was mostly what appeared to be endless plains of low rolling hills and lots of sagebrush. As he continued further south, the landscape changed to irrigated farmlands and the foothills became much closer. Traffic became much heavier after he reached the outskirts of Ft. Collins and continued to be heavy as he traveled further south.

Kit took the Route 52 exit west off Interstate 25 and headed for Boulder. As he drove west, he could see more and more of the snow-topped Rocky Mountains that stretched beyond the foothills. They seemed to go on and on as far as he could see. A lone cowboy mounted on a big bay horse was riding along a fence bordering the highway and Kit waved at him. The cowboy waved back.

Route 52 ended just in front of a huge IBM plant. Kit turned south on State Highway 119 and was soon in Boulder, a college town with a population of about 100,000. The city was nestled at the base of the foothills and behind the south part of the city were some unusual flat rock formations that made up that portion of the foothills.

Kit used his GPS to find the Boulderado Hotel. The hotel was located in the central business district and was a combination of the old hotel and a new addition. Both were built with a red colored brick. When Kit pulled up to the front entrance, a valet rushed forward to assist him and to park his truck. Kit wasn't used to giving his truck keys to anyone and this took him by surprise. The valet assured him his truck would be safe, and he gave Kit a receipt for his keys.

When Kit entered the lobby of the hotel he noticed it was very old fashioned with a balcony around the lobby area and the ceiling of the lobby was two stories up and made of stained glass. Kit was impressed. After Kit checked in at the main desk, a bellhop led Kit to his room and carried his overnight bag. After explaining the heating and cooling system to Kit, the bellhop left when Kit handed him a five dollar bill as a tip. Kit looked around his spacious room. It featured a King sized bed and what looked like antique furniture. The bathroom was good sized. Kit unpacked his overnight bag and put his toilet kit in the bathroom.

He found a place to plug in his iPad and his cell phone and sat on the bed by the hotel room phone. After reading the instructions, he called the cell phone number that Shirley had given him.

He got a busy signal and turned off his phone. Kit had made good time, and he decided to take a look around downtown Boulder.

Half an hour later he returned to the hotel and checked with the desk clerk for the name of a good restaurant. The clerk recommended a restaurant which was conveniently located in the hotel.

"That's the best restaurant in town?" asked Kit.

After looking around to see if anyone was within earshot, the clerk recommended Jill's restaurant in the St. Julian Hotel. Kit thanked her and walked out to the front of the hotel where the valet stand was located. After giving the valet his ticket and another five dollar tip, his truck was quickly brought around to the stand.

Kit flipped on his GPS and found the location of the Boulder Hospital. He knew Shirley would be working until five o'clock and a glance at his watch told him it was a little after four.

"What the heck," thought Kit. "If the mountain can't come to you, go to the mountain."

CHAPTER THREE

KIT PULLED INTO THE HOSPITAL parking lot and parked the truck. He walked across the mostly full parking lot and into the entrance of the hospital. He stopped at the front desk and told the attendant he was there to see Nurse Shirley Johnson.

The attendant pecked away at her computer and said, "Nurse Johnson is on duty until five, but I can page her. If you'll have a seat over there in the waiting area, I'll see if she is free to come down and see you."

"Thank you, ma am," replied Kit, and he took a seat in the waiting area where he could see the entrance doors as well as the elevators to the right.

Meanwhile, Nurse Shirley Johnson was just finishing her rounds of post-surgery patients when her friend and fellow nurse Kyla ran up and grabbed her by the arm.

"What's up, Kyla?"

"I just got a call from the front desk and there is some tall, good looking dude in a cowboy hat and cowboy boots here to see you."

Shirley smiled and actually felt herself blush. "That must be Kit. I was expecting him, but not this early and not here."

"You were expecting Clint Eastwood? How in the world do you know this guy?"

"It's a long story, but I met him when I was on vacation in Wyoming last summer, and he just happened to have gotten shot."

"Shot! You mean like shot with a gun?"

"That's usually how it happens, Kyla. You'll have to excuse me. I need to head downstairs to see someone."

Kit had settled into a rather uncomfortable chair in the waiting area of the hospital lobby. As he looked around, he noted that Boulder sported a much nicer and more modern building than the last hospital waiting room he had been in during a trip to South Carolina. He looked over the months old and dog eared selection of magazines on the table in front of him, but he was too nervous to concentrate and decided people watching in the lobby would be more entertaining and easier on his nerves.

Kit heard the ding of an elevator arriving and looked over to see what he had been waiting for. Striding out of the elevator was a tall willowy attractive blonde. She was dressed in light blue scrubs that seemed to accentuate her brilliant blue eyes sparkling with the reflection of the room's overhead lights. She had definite Scandinavian facial features. Her almost white blonde hair was pulled back in a pony-tail, just as Kit remembered her. As Shirley caught sight of a rapidly rising Kit, she smiled and her smile seemed to add more light to the already brightly lit room.

Kit found himself feeling tightness in his throat and dryness in his mouth. Shirley looked like some Nordic princess.

As they approached each other in the lobby, both of them seemed to feel a sense of awkwardness. It was like they couldn't decide if they were supposed to shake hands politely or hug each other with enthusiasm. While Kit's brain was trying to decide what to do, Shirley solved his problem by opening her arms and giving Kit a hug.

"Wow. You look terrific," said Kit.

"Thank you, but I look a sight after an eight hour tour on the ward and I know it," said Shirley with a smile.

"If that's true, I'd have to wear dark glasses to see you when you're all spiffed up."

Shirley laughed and began to blush.

Her laugh was light and pleasant to Kit's ears.

"What are you doing here so soon? I wasn't expecting to hear from you until tonight."

"I made good time and had no weather or traffic problems," said Kit. He tactfully left out the fact that he was pushing the speed envelope all the way from Wyoming.

"How's the shoulder?"

"The shoulder feels fine, thanks to you."

"I had very little to do with how your shoulder feels, Kit."

"I think you had a lot to do with it."

Shirley looked at her watch and frowned. "I have to get back to my ward. I'll see you at my apartment at seven o'clock?"

"I'll be there. It's really good to see you again under much better circumstances, Shirley."

Shirley smiled at Kit. "I'm glad to see you again, no matter what the circumstances."

She leaned in and gave him a quick kiss on the cheek, and she turned and disappeared into the elevator.

Kit stood there in the lobby and touched his hand to the cheek she had just kissed. He looked at his watch. He had two and a half hours before he was to pick Shirley up for dinner. It would be the longest two and a half hours he had ever spent.

CHAPTER FOUR

KIT ARRIVED AT THE OLD house on Pine Street at five minutes before seven o'clock. The old house was in good condition and had been subdivided into two apartments. Kit found the doorbell under a small sign that said "Anderson/Turner."

Kit rang the doorbell and heard what sounded like footsteps on a stairway. Pretty soon the door was pulled open and he was confronted by a short, dark haired girl who looked to be in her late twenties. She wore jeans and a sweatshirt with "The University of Colorado" emblazoned on it. She greeted Kit with a smile and a cheerful hello.

"I assume you are Mr. Kit Andrews," she said with a grin.

"You are correct, ma'am."

"I feel like I'm a little young to be called ma'am, but as I remember, that's how all you cowboys talk. Is that right?"

"Yes, ma'am."

"Please, call me Leslie and skip the ma'am's, please."

"Yes ma---, Leslie," said Kit as he caught himself.

Leslie smiled as she shut the door behind them and led Kit up the stairs to a second floor apartment. The old house was updated, but it still featured tall windows and the high ceilings. The apartment was furnished tastefully, but it was obvious some of the furniture had been recycled from somewhere else.

Leslie pointed to a large easy chair and said, "Make yourself at home. Shirley will be out in a few minutes." Leslie then disappeared through a doorway, closing the door behind her.

Kit looked around and saw a mixture of old and new. The furniture was old, but in good condition. The hardwood floor had a bright shine to it and featured two large area rugs in earth tones. A large flat screen television and a fairly inexpensive sound system dominated the end wall of the room. Kit could see trees and the side of a neighboring house through the nearest windows. There was a bookcase filled with books and CD's along the other end wall of the room.

Suddenly the door opened and Shirley stepped through the doorway. She still had her hair in a pony-tail but had changed to a blue and white striped summer dress that ended about four inches short of her knees. She wore sandals on her feet.

Kit immediately stood and tried not to stare at the lovely vision he beheld in front of him.

"You look terrific," he finally managed to blurt out.

Shirley grinned and despite her best efforts she blushed.

"So have you figured out where we're going to dinner?"

"I made reservations for Jill's at the St. Julian Hotel," said Kit. "I hope that's ok with you.

"Ok! That's a terrific place. I've never been there, but I have heard nothing but good things about it. Are you sure you want to go there? I hear it's very pricey."

"Hey, I owe you big time. Price is pretty irrelevant considering what you did for me."

"I didn't do anything any trained nurse wouldn't have done. I'm just happy that you're healed and ok. You are fully recovered aren't you?"

"Good as new. Maybe better."

"Great. Let me grab my jacket. It can get chilly in Boulder after the sun goes down."

"Just like in Wyoming," said Kit.

The sun was just starting to set behind the Flatirons as Kit pulled up onto the circular drive in front of the St. Julian Hotel. He had no sooner stopped the truck when a uniformed valet appeared just outside the driver's side door. Kit rolled down his window and gave his name to the valet who took his truck keys and gave Kit a numbered receipt for his truck. Kit exited the truck and quickly went around the front of the truck and opened the door for Shirley.

Kit asked the valet where the restaurant was located and the man smiled and pointed to a door at the east end of the circular drive. Kit confirmed his reservation with the hostess, and he and Shirley were quickly led to a table for two located right next to a street-side facing window. Kit held Shirley's chair out for her to be seated and then retreated to his chair.

"This is great," said Shirley. "Now we can get some people watching in along with our dinner."

Kit was a little confused until he looked out the window, and sure enough there were all kinds of people on the sidewalks on both sides of the street. A majority of the people Kit saw were younger, but there were plenty of older couples walking by as well.

The waiter brought glasses of water and menus as well as a basket of fresh bread and butter. Kit asked Shirley about what kind of work she did as a nurse, and she gladly obliged. They were interrupted by the waiter, and they realized they had not even opened their menus. Shirley told the waiter to come back in a few minutes and picked up her menu. Kit followed suit and after a couple of minutes, Shirley said, "I think I'll have the salmon."

"That's something we don't see much of in Kemmerer. I eat a little trout, but I can't remember when I had salmon. I think I'll have the salmon as well."

The waiter came and they gave him their orders and Shirley continued with her stories about her job. Kit hung on every word.

Kit asked about Shirley's family and learned that she was raised on a ranch near Montrose, Colorado, located on what she referred to as the Western Slope. Her mother and father were both still on the ranch and she had three brothers.

"Three brothers?"

"I learned to fight to survive early," said Shirley with a smile.

"Why did you decide to become a nurse?"

"I decided I would like to try to do something good in this world that always seems to focus heavily on the bad."

Kit was impressed with her answer to his question.

Their orders came and their conversation was interrupted by some serious attention to their meals. Kit had forgotten how little he had eaten and he was really hungry.

When the waiter asked about dessert, Kit was about to say no when Shirley cut him off and said, "We'll each have bananas foster."

The waiter left and Kit turned to Shirley. "What the heck is bananas foster?"

"Trust me. You'll love it."

The waiter came and prepared the desert tableside, and Kit's eyes got big when he saw their dessert on fire. Shirley laughed at him. The dessert was delicious.

The waiter came with the bill, and Kit paid it and left a generous tip on the table. He helped Shirley from her chair and grabbed her jacket for her, and they left the restaurant.

As they got outside, Shirley put her hand on Kit's chest. He looked at her with a puzzled expression on his face.

"Before we get your truck back, let's go for a walk and see a little of the Pearl Street Mall."

"The Pearl Street Mall?"

Shirley explained how they converted Pearl Street in downtown old Boulder to a pedestrian mall and how popular it was. Indeed, the Boulder Pearl Street Mall was the most popular pedestrian mall in America. She further explained the mall housed not only shops and restaurants, but also buskers who were licensed by the city.

"Buskers?"

"Buskers are entertainers. They play music, they dance, they walk tightropes, they juggle, and one can even tell you your hometown if you give him the ZIP Code."

"Really!"

"Absolutely."

"How do they get paid?"

"They all have hats, cups, or bowls in front of them for you to toss money in if you like what they are doing."

"Let's go see some buskers."

Shirley had been right on the money in her explanation. The pedestrian mall was crowded with people of all types and descriptions. There were buskers, as she had described, and there were play areas for children with metal statues of animals that they kids could play on and there was a flat, ground level fountain made of a steel grate with round holes in it that periodically shot water up in the air. The water jets changed every few seconds and children ran around on it trying to either avoid the water or get wetter.

One part of the mall was in front of the county courthouse, complete with a civil war statue. Kit's favorite stop was the Rocky Mountain Chocolate Factory for some very expensive and very delicious pieces of chocolate.

"Not as good as bananas foster, but darn good," said Kit. Shirley smiled in agreement.

"Boulder is a very diverse city. It's also a very liberal place. You can be whoever you want to be and express your feelings and beliefs freely, as long as you don't try to force them on someone else," said Shirley.

"So that explains the crazy outfits and the wild looks?" said Kit.

"Pretty much," said Shirley.

They continued their walk down the mall, stopping now and then to look in a shop window or to listen to some buskers play music.

One busker who stood out to both of them was a young boy about eleven or twelve years old who was playing the violin. The boy was very good and his music was haunting. When the boy finished his song, Kit and Shirley clapped their hands in applause as did the rest of the small audience the boy had drawn with his music. Kit slipped a five dollar bill in the boy's collection bowl, and he and Shirley continued their walk.

When they reached the west end of the mall, Shirley looked at Kit and said, "Had enough of the mall?"

"I think I've seen enough."

"Let's go back to the hotel and get your truck. This tour of Boulder isn't over yet."

They turned and began to walk back down the three block long pedestrian mall when Kit suddenly stopped.

"Is there something wrong?"

"No. I just heard what sounded like French being spoken."

Shirley looked at Kit and laughed. "Boulder is a very cosmopolitan place. You can usually hear at least six foreign languages when you walk down the Pearl Street Mall. We get people from all over the world who come here to study, to live, to train, and to just hang out."

"This is a little different than Kemmerer," said Kit.

Shirley put her hand on his arm, and they continued down the mall.

They walked back to the hotel and retrieved Kit's truck and Shirley directed him to turn right on Pine Street.

"What's so special about this street?" asked Kit.

"Just be patient and you'll see. Okay, stop here."

Kit stopped the truck and looked to where Shirley was pointing. He saw an old Victorian house with lots of gingerbread trim.

"Do you recognize the house?"

Kit looked at the old two-story Victorian house that looked like it was brand new.

"I don't think so."

"Do you remember the television series called Mork and Mindy?"

"Not the original, but I did see it on reruns. Oh, yeah, I get it. This was the house they supposedly lived in on the second floor."

"You got it," said Shirley with a laugh. "Now drive back to Ninth Street and turn left."

Kit did as instructed and was soon directed to pull over and park the truck. Shirley got out of the truck and Kit quickly followed her to where she stood on the sidewalk.

"This is Columbia Cemetery. We're here to visit the grave of someone you should know."

"Who would I know buried here," thought Kit as he followed Shirley into the cemetery.

They walked for almost a block when Shirley stopped in front of a low grave marker made of red granite. Kit looked down and read the name on the stone.

"Tom Horn?"

"Mr. Horn was a gunfighter who worked for the big cattlemen in Wyoming and he was found guilty of murder and hanged in Cheyenne, Wyoming, in 1902. His brother drove a beer wagon in Denver, and he lived in Boulder. When Tom Horn was hanged, his brother went to Cheyenne to claim the body and brought it here to be buried."

"How do you know all this?"

"I was born and raised in Colorado and my father made sure all of us grow up proud to be Westerners. Every night he used to read us a story about the history of the West and especially Colorado and Wyoming."

Kit looked at Shirley in the growing gloom of the cemetery and could see the sparkle in her eyes. He knew sincerity when he saw it.

"What's next on the agenda?"

"Continue driving south on Ninth Street until you get to Baseline Road and then turn right."

Kit followed her directions and she explained that Baseline Road was once the southern border of what was known as the Dakota Territory before there were many western states. Baseline Road led them up to the top of Flagstaff Mountain, a city park that overlooked Boulder from the west.

It was getting dark out by the time Kit parked the truck in the lot at the top of Flagstaff Mountain. He could see the lights of the city below them. He and Shirley exited the truck and walked over to the low stone wall that marked the end of the parking lot. From there they could see the lights of Boulder and the lights of other towns and homes as well as the lights of the cars and trucks on the busier highways. It was a spectacular view.

'Have you ever heard of the curse of Chief Niwot?" asked Shirley.

"No. Who was Chief Niwot?"

"Niwot was a chief of the Northern Arapahoe Indians. They were the tribe that lived and hunted here before the white settlers arrived. He was friendly to the new settlers and tried to keep peace between his people and the whites. Niwot means left hand in Arapahoe and many places in the county are named after him including Left Hand Canyon and Left Hand Creek, as well as the village of Niwot."

"So what was the curse?"

"Niwot said that anyone who came here was doomed to return. I went to school here and after I graduated I got a job in Denver, but as soon as there was a job opening in Boulder, I took it."

"Was it the right move for you?"

"I love it here, but sometimes the ultra-liberals and the kooks get to me, and I need to find some open space to breathe. That's why I was in Wyoming on vacation when I ran into you and your father."

Kit was silent when Shirley mentioned his father.

"Is something wrong, Kit?"

"You mentioned my father. That kind of hit home."

"Why?"

Kit found himself pausing before relying to Shirley. His throat had gotten tight and for some reason his eyes had begun to water.

"He and my mother were divorced when I was very young. She raised me, but she told me my father had died. I never knew he was alive until I accidently stumbled on the town of Kemmerer. I met good friends of his there and found out he had lived in Kemmerer and had a place there. My father had been missing for several years. He had failed to come back to Wyoming after he went to Europe on a job."

"A job in Europe. What kind of job?"

"Apparently he did a lot of contract work for the government. Secret stuff that he never talked about."

"What happened to him?"

"He got caught and was kept in a private prison for over a year. Somehow he escaped and made his way back to the U.S. When he showed up at Dutch Joe's Guard Station near the Wind River Mountains, it was the first time I had seen him since I was a baby."

"Oh my God! I had no idea," said Shirley.

"The first time you saw him was when you'd been wounded?"

"Well, they say things happen in threes."

"What do you mean?"

"That day I met my father for the first time in twenty some years, I got shot, and I met you."

"I don't know if I like being compared to getting shot, but I'm ok with being compared to seeing your father after all those years."

Kit laughed.

"Are we done or is there more I should see?"

"We have one more stop. Go east on Baseline until you get to Broadway and then turn south."

Kit drove as instructed and soon they were passing some imposing looking government buildings on their right.

"What are those buildings?

"Those house the U.S. Government's Bureau of Standards. That's where the atomic clock is located."

A few minutes later Shirley had Kit slow down and then had him turn west on Table Mesa Drive. They drove past a shopping center to the south and then slowly through a well-built residential area. As they drove Kit sensed that they were gaining in elevation. Finally they came to the end of the residential area and entered a broad meadow that led up to the Flatirons. The road twisted through the meadow and headed to the top of a mesa.

At the top of the mesa were some tall and strange looking buildings. Shirley had him drive past the buildings to a large parking lot and they drove to the end of the lot and parked. From there they had another great view of the plains and could see the lights of cars on Highway 36 that linked Boulder with Denver via Interstate 25.

"What the heck is this place?" asked Kit.

"This place is called NCAR. That stands for the National Center for Atmospheric Research. This is where they study the weather all over the world and where a lot of the data is obtained for scientists to be able to predict what the weather is supposed to do next."

Kit could see that the buildings were several hundred yards higher than the homes below them.

"Why is it so high up and isolated from the rest of Boulder?"

"I have no idea. It was done before I came here to attend CU. I do know that it is the only construction that has been allowed above the blue line."

"What's the blue line?"

"The City of Boulder has an imaginary line that keeps anyone from building anything above it so it protects the beauty of the foothills that flank the city. They manage that by refusing to provide sewer and water services above that line."

"But they allowed this to be built?" asked Kit as his swept his arm toward the tall buildings in front of them.

"This is a piece of land owned by the federal government. I am sure this was some sort of compromise after a bitter fight between the city and the Feds."

"I have to admit it is a beautiful location and the buildings are impressive."

"This site was used to shoot part of the movie, *Sleeper*, with Woody Allen."

"I must have missed that movie."

"You didn't miss much," said Shirley with a laugh.

"Where do we go next, Miss Anderson?"

"This is the end of the tour. Let's head back to my apartment."

CHAPTER FIVE

KIT PARKED THE TRUCK ON the street in front of Shirley's apartment and got out and opened the passenger door for Shirley. The night air was warm and there was a slight breeze as he walked her up to the ground level door to her apartment and waited while she unlocked the door.

"Would you like to come up?" asked Shirley.

"Absolutely," replied Kit.

Kit paused and looked at Shirley. "You mentioned on the phone that you had something you wanted to talk to me about."

"Actually there is and it has to do with my roommate, Leslie. She has a big problem and needs more help than I can provide."

"She does?"

"I should warn you that Leslie asked me if she could talk to you. I hope that's all right with you."

"Not a problem," said Kit.

When they entered the second floor apartment, they found Leslie sitting on the couch watching television.

Leslie turned it off with the remote.

"How was the dinner?" asked Leslie.

"It was excellent. We ate at Jill's at the St. Julien."

"I heard that was a great restaurant, but I've never been there."

"Neither had I until tonight. Most of my previous dates took me to exotic places like The Sink and Old Chicago."

Kit just stood there not saying a word, but he was blushing in spite of his efforts not to.

"I just made a pot of coffee. Is anyone interested in a cup?" asked Leslie.

"That sounds great. Let's sit at the kitchen table, or whatever it is that we have that passes as our kitchen table. I'll get the mugs," said Shirley.

Kit allowed himself to be ushered in to a tiny kitchen with a small old round wooden table and three mismatched wooden chairs. The table showed dents and traces of old paint in cracks in the table's surface.

Kit sat down on the chair that looked to be the sturdiest of the three and Shirley brought three mismatched mugs to the table and Leslie produced a fresh pot of coffee.

"Do you take anything with your coffee, Kit?" asked Shirley.

"I usually take cream and sugar, if you have it."

"I have sugar and 2% milk. Will that do?"

"That'll be fine. I can remember days herding sheep when I used condensed milk from a can."

"That doesn't sound very appealing," said Shirley, with a grimace on her face.

"Out on the mountains you use what you have and learn to be grateful for it."

Both women looked at each other, and each made a face of disgust.

After the coffee was poured and Kit had taken a couple of sips he sensed something was up because both women had been silent and Leslie looked particularly apprehensive. She looked at Shirley, and Shirley gave her a nod of her head.

"Kit, Leslie has something she would like to ask you, and I told her it would be all right. I don't want you to think this is why you're here, but Leslie has a problem that she thinks you might be able to help her with."

The silence broken, Kit put down his mug and sat back in his chair, waiting for Leslie to speak.

"Look, Kit. You don't know me and I probably have no business asking you for anything, but I have nowhere else to turn."

Kit leaned forward in his chair, as he could sense what sounded almost like panic in her voice.

"This is about my brother Leon Turner. Leon is two years older than me, and he works as a teacher in a high school in Longmont in the St. Vrain School District. He was a history major in college, and he has always been a bit of a dreamer. Each summer vacation for the past two years, he has taken a month off and gone to Arizona to do some exploring. He called it exploring, but the truth is he has had a bug for years about treasure hunting. This summer he went to a place called Skeleton Canyon in southeastern Arizona, and he never came back."

"When was he supposed to get back from this trip?" asked Kit.

"About six weeks ago."

"Have you talked to local law enforcement down there?"

"Almost daily and they are getting tired of me calling."

"What have they told you?"

"They found his car, a 1999 Subaru, parked near a place called Apache, Arizona. It was parked next to where a gate closes off the entrance to the canyon. It's called Skeleton Canyon Road."

"Did they find any clues in the car?"

"They found nothing but a suitcase in the car. The car was covered with dust, and it hadn't been disturbed."

"Did they conduct a search?"

"Yes, they did. They sent two deputies to search the canyon, and they found no trace of Leon."

"How long ago was this?"

"About a month ago."

"You mentioned a gate on this Skeleton Canyon Road. Why would there be a gate on a public road? Or is it a private road?"

"My understanding is that the road is a county road, but the landowners on both sides of the road to the canyon became angry with the constant flow of illegal immigrants and drug smugglers through the canyon and onto their property and the lack of action by the local authorities to do anything about it, so they closed the road with a locked gate in 2005."

"And the county did nothing about it?"

"Apparently not. I never got a clear answer about the gate and the road. I got the feeling the deputy didn't want to talk about it."

Kit sat back in his chair and took another sip of coffee. Now he knew why Leslie had looked and sounded so upset. Kit looked up at Leslie. "What do you want from me?"

"Shirley told me about how she met you and what happened up in the Wind River Mountains in Wyoming. She and I Googled your name and we came up with stories about what you did to find that gold in South Carolina and how you helped find that long lost pilot in Wyoming. I hate to ask you for help, Kit, but I am out of options and I don't have any money to speak of so I can't afford to hire a private detective."

"You looked me up on Google?"

"Yes, we did," said Shirley.

Kit looked over at Shirley and saw a hint of a smile on her face.

Kit turned his attention back to Leslie. "Do you have any information on this Skeleton Canyon and can you give me a list of who you talked to down in Arizona along with their phone numbers?"

"Yes, I do and I can."

Leslie rose from her chair and disappeared into her bedroom. When she returned, she had a fat cardboard file tied with a string.

"In this file are my notes from talking to the sheriff's office in Arizona and all the information I could dig up about Skeleton Canyon from the internet."

Kit took the file from her and placed it on the table in front of him.

"Do you have any idea of just what your brother was looking for in Skeleton Canyon?"

Leslie thought for a moment and then she began to explain what she knew about Skeleton Canyon.

"Most people know about Skeleton Canyon because it is the place where the Apache Geronimo and his band surrendered to General Miles. The canyon got its name from the large number of bones that kept coming to the surface in parts of the canyon. The canyon runs east and west for about six miles. The eastern end is in New Mexico and the western end is in Arizona. It is located about thirty-five miles north of the Mexican border. For many years the Apache used it as a thoroughfare through the Peloncillo Mountains as they journeyed back and forth between Mexico and Arizona. The canyon is located in Cochise County, Arizona."

"The legend of the treasure has to do with a Mexican burro train of silver bullion that was coming from Mexico and passing through the canyon. Two members of the Clanton gang from near Tombstone, Arizona, heard about the burro train and they ambushed the train in the canyon. They killed all the Mexicans and several of the burros. They were not the brightest guys and had no way to move all the silver with the remaining burros. They used the surviving burros and moved the silver to a side canyon and buried it and made several trips until they had moved all the silver. Then they killed the remaining burros back where they had ambushed the Mexicans. They decided to keep quiet about their ambush until things had quieted down."

"Unfortunately one of the two got drunk and bragged to the other members of the Clanton gang about what he had done, and they demanded to be cut in on the silver. He refused and in trying to force him to talk, the gang killed him. They knew about his partner and when they went to confront him, a gunfight broke out and he was killed. So now no one was left alive who knew where the silver was buried, and that is the basis of the legend of the treasure in Skeleton Canyon."

"Sounds a lot like a fairy tale," said Kit.

"I would agree except for one thing," replied Leslie.

"What is that?" asked Kit.

"One of the two men wrote a letter to his sister. In the letter he told her what he had done and said that if anything happened to him, she could have the silver and he left directions as to where it was buried."

"What happened to this letter?" asked Kit.

"It is currently on display in the Arizona History Museum in Tucson."

"So why hasn't someone used the letter to find the silver?" asked Kit.

"Because one of the major landmarks the outlaw used was a peak that he and his partner had given a name to, but no one has ever heard of a peak with that name."

"It still sounds like some big hoax," said Kit.

"It may be a hoax, but my brother believed it and he was no dummy."

"Did your brother have a lot of experience with living in the wilderness? Asked Kit.

"He did a lot of backpacking and camping. He was no stranger to being in the back country, but I wouldn't call him a survivalist or an outdoor expert."

"Did he have any military training or experience?"

"No. He never served in the military. I think he was in the Boy Scouts, but that was it."

Kit looked at his watch. "It's getting late and I know Shirley has to work tomorrow, so I'll take this file back to the hotel with me and look it over. I'll come back tomorrow after you're home from work and let you know what I think."

Kit stood and Leslie gave him a hug.

"Thank you for listening. This means a lot to me," said Leslie.

"Let's wait until tomorrow to see if there is anything to thank me for," replied Kit.

Shirley walked with Kit to the door.

"Thank you for listening to Leslie. I am sorry to do this to you, but she's my friend and she needs help I can't give her."

"She's lucky to have a friend like you," said Kit.

Shirley put her hand behind Kit's head and pulled him down to her and their mouths met in a soft kiss.

"Thanks for coming and thanks for dinner and the evening. I had a great time, and I'd like to continue seeing you."

Kit looked surprised and Shirley followed up with a longer and more sensuous kiss that Kit would not soon forget.

CHAPTER SIX

KIT SAT BACK IN THE easy chair in his room and prepared to read the contents of Leslie's thick file on her brother and Skeleton Canyon.

He had stopped at the restaurant in the hotel and bought a large coffee to go, and he took a sip before he opened the file. First he went through the file and tried to sort the materials into several small piles. He put Leslie's handwritten notes in one pile, a couple of maps of Arizona in another pile, and pages that Leslie had apparently printed out from what she found on the internet about Skeleton Canyon and the alleged treasure in another.

By the time he had finished the coffee, he had finished reading the contents of the file. After setting the file aside, he went to his suitcase and took out a spiral notebook and a ball point pen. Then he took his iPad Air out of his suitcase and changed the settings to accommodate the hotel's wireless system.

When he had a solid signal, Kit signed onto the internet and began searching Skeleton Canyon in Arizona. There were lots of sites and information on the canyon, the alleged treasure, and other things like the Geronimo surrender site and the site of Ike Clanton's murder.

"This place has a pretty gruesome history," thought Kit.

He began taking notes as he read and when he was done, it was about one o'clock in the morning.

"Enough of this crap," Kit said and he shut down the iPad, undressed, and slipped into bed.

Kit arose at 7:00 the next morning. He showered, dressed and then went for a walk around downtown Boulder. After about half an hour, he returned to the hotel. He bought a local newspaper, the *Boulder Daily Camera*, and then went into the hotel restaurant for breakfast.

Kit drank a cup of coffee and read the paper while he waited for his breakfast to be served. The *Camera* was a pretty sophisticated product compared to the *Kemmerer Gazette*, but after reading the editorial page and the letters to the editor, it was obvious he was not in Wyoming anymore. It pretty much supported the theory that Boulder, also known as the People's Republic of Boulder, was twenty square miles surrounded by reality. Kit almost laughed out loud at the opinions of outrage expressed in the letters to the editor.

"Sometimes the truth is funnier than anything you could make up," he thought.

After breakfast, he went up to his room and fired up his iPad again. Using his notes from the night before, Kit was looking up specific items that had grown out of questions raised from the previous night's research and reading.

Kit put down his iPad and then began to write down a list of questions on his note pad. When he was finished, he then began a second page with a list of things he needed to do.

Kit took out his cell phone and after checking his list of things to do, he began making some phone calls.

His first call was to Swifty.

"Hello."

"Is your ass out of bed yet?"

"It'd be a cold day in hell when you beat me out of bed, you greenhorn tenderfoot."

"Hah. After a night of carousing you're lucky to be up by noon."

"Well, things have been a little quiet around here since you left. Why the hell are you calling me at this ungodly hour? Don't tell me you actually scored with the nurse!"

"No, I did not score with the nurse."

"Hah. I knew it. Did you even get a handshake or just a brush off at the door?"

"I did better than a handshake, but I'll tell you about that later. That's not why I'm calling."

"Don't tell me, let me guess. You're in jail."

"Nope. But I do have a job to do that would include you."

"A job! You mean work? You know how I think work is a four letter word."

"This job is to find a missing brother of Shirley's roommate."

"How did she manage to lose him?"

"She didn't. He went on a treasure hunt down in Arizona and disappeared about six weeks ago."

"Did she try the local cops?"

"Yeah, and they've had no luck, and she's getting desperate."

"Just where in Arizona was this idiot looking for treasure?"

"He was looking for treasure in a place called Skeleton Canyon."

"Skeleton Canyon! What the hell is that, some sort of Halloween Park?"

"Actually it's a pretty remote place with a pretty gruesome history. It's the place where Geronimo surrendered back in the late 1800's."

"Let me guess. You've decided we're gonna go look for this idiot."

"Pretty much."

"What do you need from me?"

"Do your Delta Force act and figure out what we need to conduct an extended search in a six mile long canyon in southeast Arizona about thirty-five miles north of the Mexican border."

"Great. Now along with rattlesnakes, scorpions, and buzzards we have to contend with illegal immigrants and drug smugglers."

"Pretty close. We need to be ready for all of the above. I'll be back on Monday about five o'clock. Meet me at my place."

"Roger. See you then."

Kit smiled as he ended the call. His partner Swifty bitched about everything, but there was nobody more reliable, especially in a tight situation.

Next Kit called Woody Harrison. Woody was Kit's father's friend and attorney and now represented Kit, as well, in all legal issues. Kit explained the basics of his plan to go to Arizona to Woody who asked a few questions, but basically listened to Kit's story. Woody was a very smart attorney and one of the reasons he was so effective was he was an excellent listener. He also had influence in all kinds of places in the federal and state governments that constantly amazed Kit.

Kit asked Woody to contact the Sheriff's office in Cochise County, Arizona to find out about access to Skeleton Canyon and to get an update on the search for Leslie's brother Leon.

Kit got back on the I-Pad and after finding the right site; he ordered both topographical maps and aerial maps of Skeleton Canyon to be sent overnight to his home in Kemmerer, Wyoming.

Then Kit got back on the phone and called his mentor, Big Dave Carlson. Big Dave had given Kit a job as a sheepherder when Kit ended up in Kemmerer, Wyoming, when he was on the run from the mob in Chicago. Big Dave had been like a father to him, and it turned out that Big Dave was a close friend to Kit's father, a man Kit had never met.

"Hello. Who the hell is this?"

Kit had to suppress a laugh. Big Dave was loud and blunt to everyone, not to mention profane.

"Big Dave. This is Kit."

"Kit! How the hell are you?"

"I'm fine. I'm in Boulder, Colorado."

"Boulder! Oh, yeah. How's the nurse?"

"She's fine, but her roommate has a missing brother, and she's asked for my help in finding him."

"Where did this lad go missin'?"

"A place called Skeleton Canyon in southeast Arizona."

"I know the place, or I've heard of it. Damn nasty place as I recall."

"You recall correctly. Not much good has ever happened there."

Kit went on to tell Big Dave the whole story and to give him his thoughts on how to proceed with a search.

"You end up looking for folks in the goddamned worst places I can think of, Kit."

"I don't pick the places and I don't look for the jobs, they just seem to find me."

"Let me guess. This gal ain't got no goddamed money."

"You are right again, Big Dave."

"Well, hell, hunting for some lad in Arizona sounds like more fun than countin' sheep. Count me in. I'll think about your plan, and tell you what I think when I see you. When are you gettin' back?"

"I'll be back on Monday afternoon about five o'clock."

"Call me then, and we'll get together."

"Thanks, Big Dave. I'll see you then."

Kit looked over his list of things to do and found he had crossed off all of them. He went over all the notes and information in the file and pulled out the maps and began to study them.

CHAPTER SEVEN

KIT ARRIVED AT SHIRLEY'S APARTMENT at a little before six o'clock on Saturday night.

Shirley was dressed in jeans and a blue top that seemed to match the color of her eyes. As usual she had a big smile for Kit.

"Ready to head out?" asked Kit.

"I was born ready," replied Shirley.

"That sounds like a Wyoming girl talking."

"I'm a Colorado girl through and through, but I really like Wyoming."

Kit just grinned and helped Shirley into his truck.

As they buckled themselves into the truck's seats, Shirley asked, "Where are we headed for? You told me to dress casual, and I don't want to be embarrassed if you are headed for some place like the Flagstaff House."

"You'll see pretty soon, and you won't be embarrassed. Trust me."

"Have you come up with a decision on whether you can help Leslie?"

Kit paused before answering while he was pulling out to pass a slower car in front of him.

"I think I can spare the time to head down to Arizona and see what I can find out. I've never been there before, so it's probably a good excuse to see the country."

"If you like sand, sage, snakes, and nasty insects along with lots of heat, then you're in for a treat."

"I learned a long time ago that it's hard to complain about something in advance of actually experiencing it."

"I'd have to agree with that. In any case, Leslie will be thrilled that someone is willing to try to help her. I have to say I am happy, but not surprised."

"Why are you not surprised? I could have said no," said Kit.

"I was pretty sure you would. I have you pegged as a stand-up kind of guy."

Kit felt himself blushing and he endured the next few moments of embarrassing silence until he could think of something half-way intelligent to say to change the conversation.

"How was your day at work?" asked Kit.

"It was fine. It seemed to go more slowly today, but I think that's because I was looking forward to tonight."

"So it sounds like I have to work hard to live up to those expectations."

"I'll reserve my judgment on that."

They rode in silence for a few minutes and finally Shirley spoke.

"Can I ask you a personal question?"

"As long as I can reserve the right to plead the Fifth Amendment."

"Fair enough. What's your father like? I met him under rather unusual circumstances and my time around him was pretty brief. Someone else seemed to be the center of my attention at the time."

Kit actually felt himself blushing.

"As I told you before, he left my mother when I was a baby, and I never got to know him. When I was a little older, my mother told me he was dead.

When I came to Kemmerer to hide out from the mob, it was by pure accident that I found out that my father had lived there for years. His two best friends were Big Dave Carlson and Woody Harrison. They used my DNA to figure out who I was. Apparently they were curious about my last name and my mannerisms, which I guess are identical to my dad's."

"So you never knew he was alive and you hadn't seen him for years until that day we met?"

"That's an absolute fact."

"So what happened when Big Dave and Woody figured out who you were?"

"They met with me and informed me that they had known my dad since they both served under him in the military. After he retired from the Army he came to Kemmerer because of his two friends and built a rather remote and private home outside of town. He continued to do contract work for the government all over the world, and on his last assignment he got caught and put in a private prison in Eastern Europe.

When I came to Kemmerer, he had been gone for several years and neither Big Dave nor Woody knew if he was alive or dead. They informed me of a trust my Dad had set up and one of the instructions was that if I ever showed up looking for him, I would be entitled to part of the trust and the right to use his home as my own.

Big Dave and Woody helped save my life, along with my best friend Swifty Olson. Since then, I've been working for Big Dave running his sheep herds and getting on-going training from Swifty."

"What kind of training?"

"I guess you would call it para-military training with firearms and bladed weapons. Along with what I would call woodcraft skills useful for surviving in the outdoors."

"How did your father get back to Wyoming?"

"He escaped from the private prison, and then he hid out in various safe houses using his contacts from years of working in Europe. He managed to get back into the U.S. without any papers by sneaking in through Mexico, which apparently is not very difficult."

"Dad made his way back to Wyoming and found out that Swifty and I were up by the Wind River Mountains and there was some kind of trouble. He went looking for us and ran across a colorful old coot named O. J. Pratt who'd met us in the mountains and had found our horses. Apparently Dad approached the ranger station from an indirect route where he could see what was going on. When he saw the trouble I was in, he used O.J. with the horses as a distraction while he set himself up as a sniper from behind some rocks. After seeing me get shot, he began taking out the bad guys with my sniper rifle. Then he took off on horseback to run down Victor Blume, the guy who shot me. That's how he ran into you at the bridge at Buckskin Crossing."

"I'll never forget that moment when I drove the Jeep up to the bridge and was confronted by this big cowboy on horseback. Your dad made quite an impression on me."

"He keeps talking about how you quickly sized things up and offered to help. He thinks you're one tough cookie."

"I was just doing what seemed right. It was the most excitement I ever experienced in my life."

"Well, we've arrived," said Kit as he pulled up in front of a stucco building next to a small park.

"Where are we?"

"We are in the small town of Frederick, and we are in front of a well recommended restaurant called Georgia Boys. They claim to have the best barbeque in Colorado, and it looks to be my kind of place."

They exited Kit's truck and went through a portal into a large court yard. There were tables and chairs in the courtyard and the walkway led to an entrance door into the restaurant.

After a brief discussion, they elected to eat out in the courtyard. The food was excellent and the atmosphere was western casual. Kit felt right at home.

"This place would do very well in Wyoming," he said.

"This place would do well anyplace," said an impressed Shirley.

After they finished their meal, they went out to the truck. The sun was falling behind the Rocky Mountains, and they both stopped on the sidewalk to take it in. Shirley leaned up and kissed Kit lightly on the lips.

"Thank you for a lovely evening, Kit."

"Hey, the evening's not over yet. Let's head back to Boulder."

In less than an hour, they pulled up in front of Shirley's apartment.

"I'm sure Leslie is nervously waiting for us," said Shirley. "I'll make coffee while you two talk."

"Sounds like a plan to me," said Kit as he helped her out of the truck, and they went up the stairs to her apartment.

Kit stayed at the apartment for almost an hour, talking to Leslie while Shirley listened. Kit had more questions for Leslie, and he took notes on a pad that Shirley produced from her desk. Satisfied he had what he needed, Kit stood up to leave.

Leslie gave him a hug and thanked him repeatedly; although Kit kept telling her he would try to find her brother and that there were no guarantees.

Shirley walked him to the door, and they kissed in the doorway. She had her arms around Kit and leaned in close to his ear.

"Be in front of the hotel at nine o'clock sharp tomorrow morning," she whispered in his ear.

"Why?" Kit started to ask, but Shirley put a finger over his lips.

"You'll find out in the morning. Sweet dreams, cowboy."

Kit walked down to his truck in a puzzled daze, and the next thing he knew he was giving the truck keys to the valet in front of his hotel.

CHAPTER EIGHT

KIT WAS STANDING OUT IN front of the Boulderado Hotel at eight forty-five the next morning. His high school football coach had called it Lombardi Time. Being at any appointment fifteen minutes early was a reference to the legendary Green Bay Packer coach who started every meeting and practice fifteen minutes before the stated time. None of his players were ever late more than once.

At exactly nine o'clock Shirley swept into the space in front of the hotel in her yellow and black Jeep Wrangler. The top was down, and she looked as gorgeous as he could imagine. She had her blonde hair in a pony-tail and she wore blue jeans, hiking boots, a University of Colorado sweatshirt with a denim jacket over it.

"Get in, cowboy. We're burning daylight."

Kit climbed into the passenger seat and had barely buckled his seat belt when the Jeep accelerated away from the front of the hotel.

"I'm glad to see you brought a jacket, cowboy, because you are going to need it."

"Why?"

"You'll see."

"Where are we going?"

"We're going to further your education about Colorado, cowboy."

Kit kept his mouth, shut knowing Shirley would tell him what the deal was when she was good and ready and not before.

They were soon out of Boulder and heading west into a large canyon. The landscape was gorgeous with a large creek flowing next to the two lane paved road. After about twenty minutes, they reached the edge of a small town. The sign on the side of the road announced they were entering someplace named Nederland.

"Nederland?" asked Kit.

"We're not stopping here," replied Shirley.

They quickly went through the small town and headed north. Kit saw a sign that proclaimed the road to be the Peak to Peak Highway.

"Peak to Peak?"

"You'll see. Be patient."

The road was at a high altitude and to Kit the air seemed even thinner than Boulder. The rocky landscape was peppered with evergreen trees and a smattering of aspen trees. The drop-off on Kit's side of the Jeep was considerable. Kit hung onto the grab bar in front of him as Shirley expertly guided the small Jeep around hairpin turns and up steep grades.

They came to a T intersection where they slowed for an upcoming stop sign. After stopping Shirley steered the Jeep to the west. The scenery became hillier and more forested. They raced past some small village on their left that a sign by the road designated as Allenspark, population 528.

Shirley slowed the Jeep and pointed to her left. Kit turned to look and there was a small, but beautiful church on top of a large rock. Behind it in the distance Kit could see some kind of large building.

"That's the Catholic Church on the Rock. Behind it is a Catholic Church retreat. The Pope stayed there when he visited Colorado a few years ago."

Soon they were descending down a steep grade and on Kit's right was a large valley.

"That is Estes Park," said Shirley.

They reached the bottom of the grade and they were entering the outskirts of the mountain town. Kit was surprised to see several large elk calmly grazing in the front yards of some houses that fronted the highway.

Kit pointed at the elk and said, "Do they stay here during hunting season?"

Shirley laughed. "They come down into town during the winter and bad weather and go back up into the high country during the summer."

"So they're tourists without any papers?"

"Something like that."

Shirley drove past the small lake in the middle of town and kept driving through part of the business district. Estes Park looked like what it really was, a typical tourist town with lots of t-shirt stores and even stores selling salt water taffy.

Finally they reached the edge of town and were out in the country with a few scattered homes and a mountainside to their right.

Shirley slowed down as they approached a spot where the road widened and went into lanes that led to small roofed booths like you might see on a toll road. The sign next to the booths proclaimed, Welcome to Rocky Mountain National Park.

"So, this is your surprise."

"No one should ever come to Colorado and not visit Rocky Mountain National Park. It's a gorgeous place any time of the year."

They drove through a small valley with several small ponds to their left. "These ponds are frequented by bighorn sheep, usually at dawn and dusk. We might see some on the way out."

After passing through the valley, they curved to the left and began a steep climb. Finally they came to a T intersection and turned to the right. After that, it was one twisting hairpin turn after another with each turn revealing another magnificent view of the park. The scent of pine wafted through the open windows of Shirley's Jeep. There were valleys, mountains, cliffs, rock formations, and tons of evergreen trees. Soon they were driving above the tree line and the views were of several mountain peaks and valleys.

"We're up about ten thousand feet and before the white man showed up, this was an Indian trail used by the Ute Indians to travel back and forth to the front range of Colorado."

"You mean like Boulder?"

"Exactly."

Soon they were heading downhill and Shirley turned into the visitor center located at the top of Trail Ridge Road.

They parked the Jeep and got out to visit the rest rooms and tour the visitor center and gift shop. The center was full of photos and useful information about the park's plant life and animal life. The gift shop was full of the usual tourist stuff.

They returned to the Jeep and headed back the way they had come. The views were no less spectacular. Soon they were back at the T intersection, but this time Shirley went straight instead of turning left back into the small canyon.

She drove for about three miles and then pulled off to the side of the road where there was a small flat area covered with gravel.

"What's this?" asked Kit.

"This is where we have our picnic," said Shirley with a grin.

They got out of the Jeep and Shirley took a picnic basket and a small cooler out of the back of the Jeep.

Kit took the basket and cooler from her, and she led the way downhill to a picnic table under a large tree a few yards from the Jeep.

Shirley opened the cooler and handed Kit a Coors Lite beer and proceeded to empty the picnic basket of its contents. She took out plates, silverware, napkins, fried chicken, potato salad, chips, and small dill pickles and pre-cut cheese cubes. She put some of everything on two plates and placed the plates in front of Kit and herself. She then took another Coors Lite beer out of the cooler and sat down opposite Kit.

"Wow! I have to say I never expected anything like this. I can't remember the last time I was on a picnic with a beautiful woman."

Shirley's eyes twinkled and she grinned and blushed.

"It seemed like the least I could do after the two great dinners you took me to."

Kit finished eating and turned around on his seat with his back to the table so he could take in the view.

"Got any more beer in that little cooler?"

"One Coors Lite coming up."

Shirley handed Kit the cold can of beer and he popped the top and took a long swig.

"I doubt that it could get any better than this."

"Well, Kit, you never know."

Later they had finished the lunch and driven back down through the park and back onto the Peak to Peak Highway. Within an hour they were back in Boulder.

When they reached the Boulderado Hotel, Shirley pulled into the long term parking lot across the street from the hotel instead of driving to the valet parking area and letting Kit off.

"Is there a reason why you are parking your Jeep here?" asked Kit.

"You'll see."

After they got out of the Jeep, Shirley reached into the back of the vehicle and pulled out a black gym bag.

"What's that for?" asked Kit.

"That's my overnight bag," said Shirley.

"Overnight bag?"

"You know, the bag you take with you when you are staying overnight somewhere beside your apartment."

"You mean . . ."

"Sometimes you can be really dense," said Shirley as she took Kit's hand and pulled him towards the entrance of the Boulderado.

"Tonight I think we should have dinner from room service."

Kit could think of no reason to disagree.

CHAPTER NINE

W HEN KIT WOKE UP MONDAY morning at six-
thirty, Shirley was already gone. He knew she
had to report to work at eight o'clock. He could still
smell her on the pillow and sheets next to him. He
rolled out of bed and found a note leaning against the
front of the flat screen television.

Dear Kit,

Thank you for everything. Looking forward to
seeing and hearing from you soon.

Love,

Shirley

Kit smiled and headed for the bathroom.

Forty minutes later Kit was in his truck and headed
back to Wyoming. He would have been a little faster,
but he had stopped to call a Boulder florist and had
ordered a dozen yellow roses to be delivered to Shirley.

He might be a little dense, but he wasn't stupid.

The miles and the time flew by and except for gas
and restroom stops, Kit didn't stop until he got back to
Kemmerer. When he had cell service in Rock Springs,
he called Swifty and arranged for them to meet for

dinner at Bootleggers in Kemmerer. Swifty was sitting at the bar when Kit entered the restaurant.

Swifty quickly slipped off his bar stool and joined Kit at a table in the back of the restaurant. Both men sat silently while Kit pretended to examine the menu.

"Okay, greenhorn, tell old Swifty what happened."

"I had a great time. Shirley is a terrific girl. End of story."

"What? You go to liberal Boulder, Colorado, for a weekend with a gorgeous blonde and that's it?"

"Like I said, end of story."

"I'm deeply hurt that you can't share one of the most exciting experiences of your life with your best friend."

"The only way you could be hurt is if the world ran out of loose women, cheap whiskey, and fast horses."

"Well, that does go without saying, but seriously, what happened?"

"I had a great time. I like Shirley a lot and we will be seeing each other again. Does that satisfy you?"

"I guess it will have to do for today. But, tomorrow is another day."

The waitress appeared and rescued Kit from having to come up with a witty retort.

"What will you boys have?" she asked.

Kit and Swifty each ordered the Cowboy Rib Eye Steak.

"Bring me and my friend a beer," said Swifty.

"I assume I'm paying tonight," said Kit.

"Of course you are. You're the dude with the money," replied Swifty.

"Have you given any thought to this expedition to Arizona, or did you forget what I asked you?"

"I did a little research on this Skeleton Canyon. You're correct about it. It has a nasty history."

"You're telling me something I already know."

Swifty ignored Kit's snide remark and kept talking.

"The place is full of things we don't like. Rattlesnakes, scorpions, tarantulas as well as no water, no shade, and it's damn hot down there. There's lots of cactus and other stuff with thorns and stickers."

"There's also another problem. The ranchers, who closed the main road into the canyon, had good reason to be pissed. Every night there are groups of illegal immigrants being guided through the canyon from Mexico by these guys called coyotes. And they're not the only ones. There are also smugglers bringing in all kinds of dope, not to mention possible terrorists from other countries."

"We need to go in prepared to defend ourselves. These are not nice people. I think two of us are not enough. We need some more guys and we need to go armed to the teeth," said Kit.

"Do you have anyone in mind to go with us?"

"I talked to Big Dave, and he said his son Thor would love to go along. He's a good hand and an army veteran. He was infantry so we can count on him."

"What about getting Big Dave or my dad to go along?"

"I asked, but they got some business deal going and they're stuck with going to Cheyenne for a while."

Swifty twirled his fork in his right hand then pointed it at Kit.

"Are three of us enough for this trip?"

"I think so, and we can always call for reinforcements if we need them."

"What else did you come up with?"

"I think we take the usual, pistols, AR-15's, your AR-10, and plenty of ammunition."

"What! No machine guns?"

Swifty looked at Kit and frowned. "You know those things are illegal, besides, they use too much ammo."

Kit laughed at Swifty's tongue in cheek reply. It was very likely that Swifty had at least one sub-machine gun in his arsenal.

"We'll need lots of ammo and good optics as well as some good quality radios. I'm not sure how well they'll work there, but we should also take at least one satellite telephone."

"How many horses should we take," asked Kit?

"I'm not sure horses will work in this canyon. If we have to search in side canyons and up canyon walls, horses aren't much good for that kind of work. I'm thinking a couple of mules for pack animals and we plan on doing a lot of walking and climbing. The canyon is only about six miles long, but I suspect we'll be doing a lot of vertical searching."

"When can you get all this stuff ready to go?"

"It's all up at your house. All we have to do is load it up."

"What about the mules?"

"They're eating hay in your corral."

CHAPTER TEN

KIT WAS UP AT SIX in the morning to the smell of bacon frying in his kitchen. He put on his robe and wandered out to the kitchen where Swifty was busy preparing breakfast.

"You're cooking?"

"I don't mind cooking when it's your food. In fact it even tastes better when I know you're paying for it. Free food is my favorite kind."

Kit groaned and headed back to his room to shower and get dressed.

In an hour they had finished breakfast and loaded up Kit's truck and after hitching a two horse trailer, they loaded up the mules along with hay and oats. They also packed several cases of bottled water and filled the large water containers at the front of the horse trailer.

Twenty minutes later, they stopped in front of Thor Carlson's house in town. Thor was a slightly smaller version of his father, Big Dave. He also had huge hands and was heavily muscled. Even in jeans and a worn denim shirt, Thor looked very much like the Viking he was named after. Thor brought his gear out of his house and after loading the gear in the back of the truck, they were on their way south.

They stopped in tiny Baggs, Wyoming, for gas and ate a quick lunch at the town's only cafe after they tended to the mules.

"How long do you think this trip will take?" asked Thor.

"We'll go as far as we can tonight and we should make it to Bisbee, Arizona, late tomorrow," replied Kit.

The trio pulled into Bisbee about five thirty P.M. the next day. Kit found a good hotel for them and a rental stable to house the mules. They ate supper at a nearby Mexican restaurant and were in bed and sound asleep by nine o'clock that night.

They met for breakfast in the hotel dining room and Kit sent Thor to pick up the mules while he and Swifty went to pay a visit to the sheriff's office.

Bisbee was a well-kept and colorful town that maintained its frontier origins. There were lots of buildings crowded into a fairly narrow mountain valley.

The sheriff's office was a bland two story stucco building that spoke little about its use or purpose. Inside it was a fairly modern office that was larger than it looked from the exterior.

After stopping at the reception desk which was manned by an older woman in a deputy's uniform, Kit and Swifty were directed to a row of chairs against the wall to wait for an available deputy.

Kit looked around the room. He saw few computers and several empty desks devoid of any personal touches to suggest they were currently manned by department personnel. While things looked neat and orderly, he began to get the feeling that the Cochise County Sheriff's office was currently understaffed.

After about fifteen minutes a short, heavy set, uniformed Hispanic man with a large Poncho Villa mustache walked up to them.

"Which of you gents is Mr. Andrews?"

"That would be me," said Kit as he rose from his chair with his hand outstretched.

"Howdy, Mr. Andrews. I'm Deputy Vegas," taking Kit's hand in his and giving him a strong handshake. Vegas had a round, unmarked face and the beginning of a beer belly.

"How about you and your friend follow me back to the conference room and tell me what's on your mind."

"Fine with me," said Kit as he and Swifty followed the deputy into a nearby conference room that held a battered old steel table and about eight equally battered old steel chairs.

As they were getting seated, the Deputy closed the door behind them and sat in a chair across the table from Kit and Swifty.

"Now, Mr. Andrews, what can I do for you today?"

"We're friends of the sister of Leon Turner, the man who went missing in Skeleton Canyon about a month ago. We'd like to know if there is any additional information on the search for his whereabouts."

Deputy Vegas sat back in his chair and took his time before answering Kit's inquiry. He seemed to study both Kit and Swifty before he answered.

"May I ask just what your connection to Mr. Turner is?"

"I've never laid eyes on the man. His sister contacted me and asked if I would come down here and see if he could be found."

"She asked you to look for him in Skeleton Canyon?"

"That's about the size of it."

"I'll be right back, Mr. Andrews," said Deputy Vegas and he left the room.

He returned in a few minutes with a legal size pasteboard file folder, which he placed on the table in front of him.

"Before I begin, Mr. Andrews, I feel it's my duty as a peace officer to warn you that a search of any kind conducted in Skeleton Canyon is both difficult and dangerous. When I say dangerous I mean deadly dangerous."

"I understand, and thank you for your advice, Deputy Vegas."

Vegas began to recite the facts of the case from the file in front of him using dates and times to designate when the sheriff's department had taken action on the case.

When Vegas was finished, he looked up from the file. "That's all we currently know about the disappearance of Mr. Turner."

"Can you tell me what you think might have happened to Leon?" asked Kit.

Vega thought for a few seconds and then began to speak. "We think Mr. Turner was a treasure hunter, based on material we found in his vehicle. We've had many treasure hunters just like him go into the canyon and get into trouble, but he's the first to disappear."

"We believe that from what we did find in his car and our search of the area that he was camping somewhere in the canyon. Lots of things could have happened to him. He could have fallen while climbing on the sides of the canyon or he could have been bitten by a rattlesnake or scorpion. He could have injured a leg or ankle and died of thirst. He could have accidently run into some drug smugglers and gotten killed."

"But why is there no evidence of a body, or even bones," asked Kit?

"I can't say. He could've been eaten by coyotes and birds. His remains could have been dragged away and scattered all over the canyon. Skeleton Canyon is a very difficult place to search, Mr. Andrews. You could sweep the canyon with a small army and easily miss a body."

"So you have no clues as to what happened to Leon?"

"Unfortunately, that's correct, Mr. Andrews."

"Can I ask how many deputies participated in the search?"

Vega's facial expression seemed to harden before he answered. "We searched the canyon with all available deputies, Mr. Andrews."

"So there is no evidence as to what happened to Leon based on your department's search?"

Vega looked a little exasperated at Kit's question. "As I told you we found nothing."

"I assume your department will have no objection to us going to the canyon and taking a look for ourselves."

"We have no objection. However, I must caution you that entrance to the canyon may be a problem for you."

"Why is that, Deputy Vega?"

"The two ranches that border the county road to the canyon have closed the road with a gate and they permit no public traffic on it."

"This is a county road?"

"Yes."

"Then it's a public road?"

"Yes."

"So how can they close a public road?"

Vega paused before answering. "They closed the road in 2005 after they had many incidents with illegals and smugglers coming through the canyon and were tired of complaining to the Border Patrol and to us and getting no results."

"Isn't this road under the jurisdiction of your department?"

"Yes, it is. However, our department is understaffed, and we have a huge county to cover. The sheriff and the county officials decided it was not worth a confrontation with the ranchers. They do not object to use of the road by our department, but they have not permitted any public use."

"Are they still having trouble with illegals and smugglers using the canyon and coming over their land?"

"The problem continues, even with the Border Patrol."

"Could illegals or smugglers have had anything to do with Leon's disappearance?"

"The canyon is a dangerous place, Mr. Andrews. It has been so since the days of the Apache and it remains so today. If you and your friend plan to search the canyon I must warn you bad people use the canyon and many bad things have happened there. If you go into the canyon, I suggest you search only in the daytime. Leave the canyon before nightfall. The canyon is not safe for anyone in the nighttime. If you get in trouble in the canyon, it will be some time before our department would be able to respond and arrive to assist you."

"I appreciate the advice, Deputy Varga. It's our intent to search for any clues as to what happened to Leon and to try to find his remains. Whatever we do find, we will share with your department. We will take precautions to protect ourselves from any dangers we might find in the canyon. Thank you for your help, Deputy Varga."

With that, Kit rose and extended his hand. Deputy Varga also rose and shook Kit's hand.

Ten minutes later Kit and Swifty were back at their hotel where Thor joined them in Kit's room.

"Well, what do you make of our little chit-chat with Deputy Vegas, Kit?"

"I think the Sheriff's Department of Cochise County is understaffed and spread very thin over a very large and rough country. I have no doubt that they searched the canyon, but how thoroughly they searched is another matter."

"Deputy Vegas did not look to be in the best shape to be climbing up canyon walls to do any searching."

"No, he didn't. But from what I've read and seen, I think this search will be tough and grueling for all of us as well. My dad warned me to not underestimate this kind of country. Relax too much and it can kill you."

"So what do we do next?"

"I think we need to circulate a bit and talk to a few locals and try to get a read of what is really the best way to get into the canyon. We can take the direct route, but I think that invites some confrontation we might not want," said Kit.

"So where should we circulate?" asked Thor.

"We hit the usual places. We hit the barber shops, the coffee shops, and a few bars as well as the stable and any feed stores."

"I'll start with the bars," said Swifty.

"Why am I not surprised," said Kit.

"I'll hit the stable and the feed stores," said Thor.

"That leaves me with the barber shops and coffee shops. Let's get moving. We can meet back here about five thirty this afternoon. Everybody agreed?"

Thor and Swifty nodded their heads and a few minutes later the door slammed on an empty hotel room.

Kit found a barber shop a block and a half from the hotel. As he stepped into the small shop an older man who had been sitting in one of the two barber chairs reading the paper, got up and set the paper aside.

"What can I do for you today, mister?"

Kit looked around the otherwise empty shop and said, "Actually I'm new in town, and I was wondering if I could get a little advice from you?"

"Haircuts are ten bucks, but advice is free. My name is Fred. Fire away."

Kit stepped forward and shook Fred's outstretched hand.

"I'm Kit Andrews from Kemmerer, Wyoming."

"Good to meet you, Kit," said Fred.

"I'm here to look for a missing friend who disappeared in Skeleton Canyon about a month ago."

"Oh, yeah, that guy. I read about that in the paper. I heard they never found a trace of the man except for his car."

"That's what I understand as well."

"So what kind of advice do you need from me?"

"I'd like to get into the canyon and look for Leon or any clues that might help the family understand what happened to him. I understand Skeleton Canyon Road is gated and locked and no public transit is allowed by the ranchers."

The barber sat back into his barber chair and motioned for Kit to take a seat on one of the chairs against the wall.

"What you heard is correct. I think that happened back in 2005 and the county boys are not up to forcing the road open. They even got pressure from a lot of hunters who can't get up to the canyon from the Arizona side."

"Is there another way into the canyon?"

"Not if you want to take a vehicle into the canyon. Skeleton Canyon Road is the only improved road I'm aware of."

"What about on horseback or hiking in?"

"You might be able to use horses if you were to come in from the New Mexico side of the Canyon. Going that way is the longest way into the canyon and the roads in that area ain't worth really calling them roads. But horses wouldn't be much use in the side canyons and going up the canyon walls and into the caves and such."

"There are side canyons?"

"Yep, there are. If you go in from the west side you go through the Devil's Kitchen and then to the south you go by Pony Canyon and then further on also to the south is Pine canyon. It's pretty rough country."

"How about going into the canyon on foot?"

"You can hike in, but it is a tough hike and the problem is you have to haul all your water into the place because there ain't no water in Skeleton Canyon."

"So, what is the best place to try to hike into the canyon?"

"There might be others, but the best way I know of is to go down to Douglas, Arizona. Do you know where it is?"

"Yes, I do. It's a town south of here right on the border with Mexico."

"That's right. Today Douglas looks more Mexican than American for my taste, but that's where you need to go."

"So I get to Douglas, and then where do I go?"

"You find Fifteenth Street and you take it to the north edge of Douglas, and it turns into Skeleton Canyon Trail. You can go so far in a vehicle, and then you have to hoof it the rest of the way."

"Can you use pack animals?"

"I've heard of using mules or burros, but not horses. The trail is too rough and too steep for horses."

"Have you ever hiked in on this Skeleton Canyon Trail?"

"Nope, can't say that I have. Last time I was in Skeleton Canyon was about fifteen years ago. I been there, and I ain't got no reason to go back."

"Why is that?"

"Skeleton Canyon is a spooky place, even in the daytime. There are a million places to hide and I can't imagine being there in the nighttime. Lots of bad things have happened in that canyon in the past and now it's even worse with all the illegals, drug runners, and plain old bandits. You couldn't pay me to go into that canyon."

"I can understand why, Fred," said Kit.

"If you do go into Skelton Canyon, don't go alone. Take plenty of water and make sure you and your party are well armed. There are all kinds of bad critters in that canyon and some of them are two legged. Stay out of the canyon at night. That's when all the foolishness happens. The Border Patrol is around the canyon and up in the air in helicopters during the day, but the bad guys rule the canyon in the night."

"Thanks for the advice, Fred," said Kit as he rose from his chair and shook hands with the old barber.

When Kit took his hand away, Fred found a ten dollar bill in his hand.

"What's this for?" asked Fred.

"I think your advice is worth as much as a haircut," said Kit as he walked out of the shop.

CHAPTER ELEVEN

A T FIVE THIRTY THAT AFTERNOON all three men made their way back to Kit's hotel room.

Before anyone could start talking, Kit held up his hand for silence.

"Before we start talking, I think we should head for a good restaurant and order dinner, then we start telling each other what each of us learned today."

There was absolutely no argument from either Thor or Swifty. Fifteen minutes later found all three seated at a table in a Mexican restaurant located about three blocks from the hotel.

A waitress dressed in a traditional Mexican outfit brought glasses of water and menus for each of the three men to their table.

"Can we talk now?" said Thor after he had taken a drink from his glass of water.

"Not yet," said Kit. "My throat is pretty dry and I'm sure Swifty is experiencing the same problem."

Swifty quickly nodded his head in agreement and grinned.

All three of them ordered margaritas with combination plates of burritos, enchiladas, and tacos. Their drinks arrived shortly after they had given the waitress their order, and they finished them quickly and ordered another round while they waited for their dinners to be served.

When they had finally finished off their large plates of food and each had polished off their third Coors beer, Kit ordered coffee for all of them and waited until the waitress returned with his order.

Kit asked both Swifty and Thor about what they had learned during their rounds that afternoon. After comparing their stories to his conversation with Fred, most of the information was the same. One common theme from everyone they had talked to was to stay out of the canyon during the night and not to go alone or unarmed.

"I'd say that was good advice," said Swifty.

"What do you think, Thor?" asked Kit.

"I was gonna suggest setting up some kind of base camp, but I decided that wouldn't work because of the lack of water and then someone would have to stay and guard the base camp so we didn't get robbed blind. What do you suggest, Kit?"

Kit took a sip of his coffee and sat the cup back down on the table.

"Old Fred the barber mentioned that there were a lot of caves up on the walls of the canyon. I think we might load up the two pack mules and hike in from Douglas on the Skeleton Canyon trail. When we get above the canyon, we can scout around for a suitable cave for a camp. During the day we leave one guy with the mules and the camp in the cave and the other two searches the canyon on foot. If we keep the search in sight of the cave, then the camp guard can be our lookout. Since we will be in sight of each other, we can use the portable radios Swifty brought."

"But that'll only work in a part of the canyon. From what you said, it's about six miles long," said Swifty.

"That means we move the camp every day to a new site until we have worked our way through the entire canyon. We spend the night up in the camp with one of us on watch all night long. Each man takes a three hour watch."

"Sounds like a plan, and we can rotate who stays in the camp so no one gets worn out searching the canyon."

"Swifty, did you bring those night vision binoculars with you?"

"Does a bear shit in the woods? Of course I brought them."

"I think they'll come in handy for whoever is standing night watch. From what I can tell, the canyon is a damn highway during the cover of night."

"Great. That way the guy on night watch can see what's going on in the canyon below us," said Thor.

"What do we do if we see groups of illegals or drug smugglers during our watch?" asked Swifty,

"We stay out of it," said Kit. "Our job here is to try to find out what happened to Leon Turner and if possible, try to find what's left of him."

"You're pretty sure he's dead?" asked Thor.

"He didn't sound like anyone who could survive in this canyon for over a month with no supplies and more importantly no water."

Kit looked around the table at his two friends.

"We know this can be dangerous. If anyone wants out, now is the time to say so."

"I'm in," said Swifty.

"Me too," said Thor.

"Then let's pay the bill and head on back to the hotel. We're gonna need our beauty rest tonight. We meet for breakfast at six and we're out of here by six thirty."

Fifteen minutes later all three men were sound asleep in their hotel rooms.

CHAPTER TWELVE

BY MID-MORNING THEY HAD REACHED the town of Douglas, Arizona. Douglas was more a scene of economic wreckage than a town. Empty storefronts were everywhere and there was a complete absence of any form of national chain store, fast food or otherwise. Everything was in disrepair and had obviously been branded with a strong Mexican overtone.

Almost every building they saw was in poor condition and trash and litter were everywhere. They drove through the decrepit town in complete silence. They found Fifteenth Street and followed it north until they reached the outskirts of Douglas and finally it dissolved into a rutted dirt road. Kit was pretty sure that road would evolve into a two-track trail before they had gone much further.

When they reached the point that the two-track became little more than a trail, they parked the truck to the side of the trail and unloaded the mules and supplies.

Swifty and Thor began placing pack saddles on the mules and then began adding the supplies in a methodical manner that showed their experience in mule packing.

Kit studied his maps and checked his personal gear and supplies in his pack as well as his weapons.

After he had locked up the truck and trailer, Kit turned to the two mule packers. "How are we fixed for water?"

"We have forty gallons on the mules and we've got another eighty gallons stored in the truck and trailer," said Thor.

"Everyone got their gear packed and checked?" asked Kit.

"All checked," said Thor

"Roger that," said Swifty. "What's our decision on exposed weapons?"

"Are the rifles and ammo stored on the mules?"

"Yes, they are, Kit."

"I think pistols in holsters should be fine as far as what we are exposing," said Kit.

"What do you mean by exposing," asked Thor.

"We always assume we are being watched, especially when we are in country we're not familiar with and others well could be. We want them to know we are armed, just not how much."

"Works for me," said Thor.

Swifty led the way as point man with Kit behind him leading one pack mule and Thor bringing up the rear with the second pack mule.

The trail was slightly elevated and rocky and they were continuously going uphill and then downhill as they climbed into and out of small ravines and ditches. They passed by occasional growths of bushes and stunted plants. Everything seemed to have a sticker or a thorn.

After about an hour of hiking, they stopped for a rest and a drink of water.

"How far have we come?" asked Thor.

Kit pulled out his map and took a reading with his portable GPS. "I'd say we are about a quarter of the way up."

Their break over, they continued on the ever challenging trail. As the mountainside became more vertical, the trail became a series of switch-backs. It was like going back and forth over the same area only slightly higher with each trip.

After another hour had passed, they paused again for a water break. The sun was high in the sky and bore down on them relentlessly with the heat continuing to increase.

They broke again for water and this time they were high enough that they sat on rocks and looked back over the terrain they had just climbed through.

"Man, this is nasty heat," said a heavily sweating Thor.

"Fortunately it seems to be affecting us more than the mules," said Kit as he examined each mule and in turn the mule's packs.

After roughly five hours, they reached the top of the mountain that represented the southern rim of their goal, Skeleton Canyon.

They tied off the mules to some mesquite bushes and flopped down on the rocky soil in the shade of a larger rock overhang. A slight breeze passed over them, and all three men seemed to relish it.

Kit drank from a canteen and passed it to Swifty. Swifty took a deep swallow of water and passed the canteen to Thor.

"I think I'll take a look see around us and make sure we are alone, and also see if I can scout out a suitable cave for us and the mules," said Swifty.

"Good idea," said Kit. "When you find something suitable, we'll move the mules down and unload them and get them fed and watered."

Almost thirty minutes passed before Swifty suddenly appeared from behind a large rock to the east of them.

"I found home, sweet home about a quarter of a mile from here," said Swifty.

"Any neighbors?"

"None you can talk to."

"Okay, Swifty. You lead the way."

It took the men about twenty minutes to move the mules along the rim of the canyon and then down slightly to a sizeable cave carved out of the upper side of the canyon.

On closer inspection, the cave was more of an area under a large rock outcropping that seemed to lie on two sizeable rocks on each side. The area under the outcropping was about fifteen feet deep and about twenty feet wide. The rock roof was about seven feet above the rocky floor.

"This will do nicely," said Kit. Thor nodded his head in agreement.

The three men busied themselves with unloading the packs from the mules. Thor took the mules to the side of the cave and fed and watered them while Kit and Swifty unpacked the things they would need to set up housekeeping in the cave.

After they finished unpacking, Kit and Swifty moved to the edge of canyon rim in front of the cave and Kit took out his binoculars and scanned the opposite wall of the canyon, as well as the rim and then looked to the right and then the left of their position on the east wall. Finally he scanned the canyon to the east and then to the west.

"I can't be sure, but I think I can see about a mile in each direction of the canyon."

He passed the binoculars to Swifty, who dutifully duplicated the same scanning pattern Kit had used.

"Two sets of eyes are always better than one," said Swifty as he finally took the binoculars down from his eyes.

"You'll get no argument from me," said Kit. "This is rugged country and there looks to be lots of caves and outcroppings where someone could hide. Even the canyon floor has a lot of trees and bushes that offer a lot of concealment. There seem to be a lot of one kind of tree, but I'm not sure what kind of tree it is."

Swifty took the binoculars and focused them on a grove of trees across the bottom of the canyon floor that was slightly northwest of their positon.

"Those would be Arizona Sycamores. I read somewhere that they grew abundantly in this canyon."

"You read somewhere? You read something about trees? My God, what's next? Swifty Olson read a book? I need to take a look and see if Hell is freezing over."

"Based on how much I've been sweating there ain't no danger of hell freezing over in this place."

Kit couldn't help himself and he burst out laughing as did Thor. Even Swifty joined in.

"Delta Boys had to know a lot about their environment, and so I naturally did some research on what we were getting ourselves into."

"Now that the mules are fed and watered, how about us?" asked Thor.

A few minutes later all three men were busy with getting utensils and food supplies out and organized.

Thor announced he was doing the cooking and soon they were setting down to a large meal of pasta in marinara sauce and garlic bread with lots of coffee.

After they cleaned up the dishes and cookware and put them away, they gathered in front of the cave with cups of coffee.

"I'll take the first three hour watch and then it will be Thor and then Swifty. Everybody okay with that arrangement?"

Both Swifty and Thor nodded agreement and the men busied themselves with laying out ground pads and sleeping bags.

Kit had insisted they use no lights to give away their presence and so Swifty and Thor crawled into their sleeping bags while it was dusk.

Kit pulled on a vest and then a canvas hunting coat. He added a stocking cap and a pair of gloves. He knew the temperature dropped when the sun went down in Wyoming and he had no reason to doubt that the same thing happened in Arizona.

After Kit found a comfortable place to sit on the rock ledge that gave him excellent views of the canyon floor both to the east and the west, he pulled out the night vision binoculars. He checked the battery power and memorized where the switch was located and sat down to watch the canyon floor as the sun began to disappear to the west.

The night sky was clear except for a few clouds and Kit's view of the stars overhead was spectacular. The moon was about half full and provided sufficient moonlight that he did not need his night vision binoculars.

As the minutes ticked by, the cold seemed to intensify. It was hard to believe that a place that seemed so hot it could boil your brains during the daylight, could be so cold when the sun went down. Kit was glad he had added the heavy coat, hat, and gloves.

Kit glanced down at his watch and saw that his three hour watch tour was almost over. He stood up and stretched out his aching muscles and walked around in a circle trying to get the stiffness out of his leg joints. Another glance at his watch told him it was the end of his watch.

He walked over to the two sleeping men and gently awakened Thor. Thor's eyes opened instantly and he looked up and nodded his head. Thor quickly got out of his sleeping bag and donned a heavy coat, beanie hat and gloves, much like those Kit wore. Once he was up and dressed he whispered in Kit's ear.

"See anything?"

Kit whispered back, "Not a thing. I had enough moon and starlight that I didn't use the night vision binoculars, but it has gotten cloudier in the past hour and you might need them for your watch."

Thor nodded agreement and he took the binoculars from Kit and moved over to where Kit has set up to watch. Thor made himself comfortable and turned on the night vision binoculars and began to scan the canyon.

Kit slipped off his coat, hat, gloves, and boots and slipped into his sleeping bag. Within minutes he was fast asleep.

CHAPTER THIRTEEN

THOR GLANCED AT HIS WATCH. Only an hour had passed. The night sky was darker with clouds and the wind had picked up slightly. He could hear nothing over the wind, and the wind brought no unusual scents to his nose.

He scanned the opposite wall of the canyon and then systematically scanned the canyon floor to his west and then to the east. Just as he was finishing his scan to the east, he saw movement on the canyon floor.

As Thor watched, he could see a line of upright figures walking in single file illuminated in the strange green light that the night vision binoculars used to turn night into day.

There were two taller figures in the lead and they were followed by about twenty shorter figures. As the group moved further west in the canyon, he could make out the difference between adults and children.

Thor rose and quietly moved to where his two friends lay sleeping.

He used his boot to nudge Kit and Swifty and both were immediately awake and alert. Thor whispered to them that he had a group moving east to west through the canyon.

Minutes later all three were dressed in coats and hats and standing by the rim of the south face of the canyon wall passing the night vision binoculars between them so each got a good look at what was happening on the canyon floor.

"What's our move?" asked Swifty.

"We move down and intercept them," said Kit.

"Why? We ain't the border patrol," said Thor.

"We need to find out if they know anything. Chances are the two in the lead are coyotes and they have been making this trip over and over. They might know something about what happened to Leon."

"What makes you think they'll talk to us?" asked Swifty."

"Because they're coyotes, and they don't know what we might do to them. We're not the border patrol, but we represent something they fear a lot more."

"What's that?"

"Three pissed off gringos with guns."

"Works for me," said Swifty.

The three made their way down a trail that Swifty had scouted when they first arrived at the rim of the canyon. Even moving down the trail in the dark, they moved much faster than the column of illegals walking on the canyon floor.

Once they reached the bottom of the trail on the canyon wall, the three men moved quickly into a grove of Arizona Sycamores and waited for the ragged column of illegals to come to them.

When the two coyotes leading the group were about fifteen yards from the trees, Kit and Thor stepped out in front of them with their guns drawn, while Swifty appeared out of the darkness on their left flank.

"Halt!"

The two coyotes halted like they had been hit with a baseball bat. At the sight of three gringos with guns, they immediately threw up their hands.

Kit and Thor took the two coyotes behind the grove of trees while Swifty kept an eye on the illegals.

Thor was fluent in Spanish, and he quickly discerned that the two coyotes were scared to death. Both of them were young Mexican men in their early twenties. The bravado they had exhibited over their submissive charges had instantly evaporated.

After about fifteen minutes of questioning the two Mexicans, Thor turned to Kit.

"These two have been though the canyon about two times a week for the past six months, and they have never seen a gringo except for us other than a couple of encounters with the Border Patrol."

"I'm not surprised, but it was worth a try," said Kit.

"What do we do with them?" asked Thor.

"We let them go."

"We let all these illegals go? They ain't called illegals for nothing, Kit."

"We're not the cops. Our job is to find a missing person, not capture illegals. Help Swifty check out the rest of them and find out if they need anything. Usually these coyotes take their money and don't even provide them with water for the trip."

Thor explained the situation to the two coyotes, who could not believe their good luck. After checking the entire group and finding no one in apparent distress, the three men stood and watched while the two coyotes got their group in a line and resumed their journey west through the canyon.

When they were out of sight, the three men retraced their steps back up to the top of the south wall of the canyon. Swifty and Kit headed back into their sleeping bags, while Thor resumed his watch.

He did not wait long before another group of ghostly figures appeared on the canyon floor coming from the east. As Thor watched them through his night vision binoculars, he determined it was another band of illegals also led by two young coyotes. This group was smaller than the first group, and Thor decided that he would get no more out of these coyotes than he had out of the first group. He elected to let them pass, and let Kit and Swifty sleep. At this rate they would be getting up every half hour and for no positive result.

Before the end of his three hour watch, Thor had seen no less than four bands of illegals pass beneath him. He was glad when his watch came to an end and after waking and briefing Swifty, Thor gratefully slid into the warm confines of his sleeping bag.

Swifty started his watch by doing a little scout around their cave to make sure they were still alone and undiscovered. Satisfied that they were alone, he settled down on the rim of the canyon wall to keep watch and to try to keep as warm as possible.

The first hour passed slowly with the only motion on the canyon floor turning out to be two small deer. The deer moved cautiously across the canyon floor, stopping frequently to sniff the air and look for any signs of danger. After about ten minutes, they disappeared into the darkness of a grove of trees.

Swifty rose to his feet and walked briskly along the edge of the canyon wall. He did this to stimulate the blood flow in his arms and legs and to get the stiffness out of his body. He also did this to keep himself as alert as possible. Delta boys did not fall asleep on post, and Swifty was no exception to the rule.

During his walk, he stopped several times to listen and to take in all of the night scents. He neither heard nor smelled anything unusual and he used his binoculars to scan the opposite canyon wall as well as the canyon floor, moving from west to east in tight patterns designed to let him carefully scan every square foot of the canyon floor.

It was during a scan of the east end of the canyon floor, that he saw the light. It was a small beam of light that softly bounced as it advanced to the west. Swifty knew immediately that he was looking at a small LED flashlight. The beam was bright, but narrow and the movement was due to the gait of the owner as he walked over the uneven surface of the canyon floor.

Swifty brought his night vision binoculars to bear on the light and soon he could see about half a dozen figures walking in a line. Three of them were leading what looked like small burros with pack saddles on them. The other three men were all carrying what looked like AK-47 assault rifles. The AK-47s were simple weapons, cheaply made, but very reliable and easy to use.

Swifty moved quickly to awaken Kit and Thor with as little noise or movement as possible.

The three men were crouched on the edge of the canyon wall taking turns with the binoculars to observe the newcomers.

"These don't look like no tourists to me," said Swifty.

"If they are, they're well-armed tourists," added Thor.

"What we have here is six heavily armed illegals smuggling drugs into the U.S. of A.," said Kit.

"Do we let them pass like the illegal?," asked Swifty."

"Those illegals were looking for jobs and a better life. These boys are criminals of the first order and well-armed criminals at that. I say we take them down."

"If we're gonna take them down, we need to upgrade our weapons from pistols," said Swifty.

"How about you, Thor? What's your vote?"

"There're six of them, but we got surprise and darkness on our side. I'm in to take them down."

"Swifty?"

"I was born for this stuff. Let's get our guns and move out."

The three moved quickly to get rifles and ammo filled magazines from their packs and they moved down the now familiar trail as quietly as possible.

Soon they were in the grove of Arizona Sycamores and had concealed themselves in the brush under the trees.

"How do you want to take them down?" Kit asked Swifty.

"I'll step out and confront them. Kit, you take the left flank, and Thor, you take the right flank. Keep low and don't reveal yourself until I raise my right hand. Everyone got it?"

Both Kit and Thor nodded their heads and moved out, keeping as low and quiet as possible.

Swifty waited in the grove of trees. He could hear the drug runners talking, and he could smell them on the night wind. Hygiene was not at the top of the criminals list of priorities.

He knew the gang had grown careless. They had probably made this trip many times without ever running into anyone, and they were probably anxious to finish the job and get out of the cold night.

Swifty decided to use a little shock value to both surprise and frighten the gang. He put his M-4 on a three shot burst with his fire selector and waited for the men and burros to get closer.

CHAPTER FOURTEEN

S WIFTY WAITED UNTIL THE FIRST man in the gang carrying the flashlight had walked to a point where he was about twenty feet in front of Swifty.

Swifty stepped out of the grove of trees and saw that the men had their heads down looking at the ground in front of them. None of them saw Swifty.

Swifty pointed his M-4 over the heads of the approaching men and pulled the trigger. A three round burst in the dead of night does several things. The sound is very loud and the muzzle flash from the barrel is exaggerated in the darkness.

The six men were both stunned and shocked and stood there as though frozen in place. Before Swifty could yell out a word, he heard a loud and strong voice yell out an order in Spanish. It was Thor.

The three armed men threw down their AK-47s and put their hands in the air. The other three dropped their lead ropes from the burros and added their hands to the collection up in the air. The burros did nothing.

Thor stepped forward with his AR-15 pointed at the six men. He gave another order in Spanish and all six men promptly lay face down on the ground.

"Check them for weapons while I cover them," Thor said to Kit.

Kit searched each man and came up with an assortment of knives and small pistols. He collected them along with the three AK-47s and several ammo magazines he found on the men.

Swifty moved past the men to collect the three burros and after a few attempts, he got the stubborn beasts to move with him past the prone gang.

Kit dumped the weapons in a pile and he and Swifty joined Thor in covering the gang with their rifles.

"What do we do with them?" asked Thor.

"Tell them they're no longer welcome in this canyon and if they return, we'll kill them," said Kit.

Thor looked at Kit in surprise, but he gave the order in loud and impressive Spanish.

"Tell them to get undressed and to pile their clothes on the ground," said Kit.

"'All their clothes?" asked Thor.

"Everything except their boots."

Thor gave the order and one of the Mexicans started to argue in Spanish.

Swifty settled the argument by firing another three round burst of .223 caliber bullets over the heads of the prone Mexicans.

That ended the argument and the six men quickly discarded their clothes and stood naked except for their boots in front of Thor, Kit, and Swifty.

"Tell them to walk back to Mexico and be quick about it. If they move too slowly, we'll shoot them," said Kit.

Thor was trying hard not to laugh out loud when he gave the order in Spanish. Few men look very tough when they are standing naked in front of you with only boots to cover their modesty and these six were no exception.

The trio stood in the darkness and watched the six Mexicans walk back to the east end of the canyon until the darkness enveloped them.

"So what do we do with this stuff?" asked Swifty as he pointed at the loaded burros and the pile of clothes and weapons.

"We load it all on the burros and take them back to the camp. We burn the clothes and turn the burros and their drug packs over to the Border Patrol as soon as we run into them," said Kit.

"What about the weapons and ammo?" said Thor.

"Spoils of war, man," said Swifty. "We keep them and put them to good use."

"Works for me," said Kit.

An hour later they were back in their cave and after securing the burros next to their mules, they dumped the clothes in a pile and put the confiscated weapons in a pack. Kit and Thor rolled up in their sleeping bags, and Swifty resumed his interrupted watch.

The next morning arrived early for the sleepy threesome as the cold of the desert night quickly morphed into the blazing heat of the sunlit day. After a quick breakfast, they decided on the plan for the day. Swifty and Thor would search the floor of the canyon, using a grid search starting from the west end of the canyon to the east end. The reasoning being that the west side was the most likely beginning of Leon Turner's treasure hunt. Kit would be the lookout and remain on the top of the canyon's southern ridge. Thor was needed in the search, as he was their only Spanish speaker. They would remain in touch by radio and would use a radio check-in every half hour since part of the time they would be out of Kit's sight.

As Swifty and Thor began their descent on the narrow trail that led down to the canyon floor, Kit fed and watered the mules and the burros. When he was finished, he pulled out the satellite phone and called the Border Patrol and reported the burros and the drugs and their location.

After Kit returned to his observation post, it was another fifteen minutes before he got a radio call letting him know Swifty and Thor had reached the floor of the canyon. Shortly after that, he located them with his binoculars. He kept them in sight as they kept to the south side of the canyon and made their way to the west entrance.

For the next three hours, Kit watched as the duo made their way back to the east of the canyon moving in a fairly narrow grid pattern. Each half hour Swifty called in with a radio check and each time they had found no sign of the missing treasure hunter.

Shortly after the last radio check, Swifty heard the loud noise of the rotating blades of a helicopter. As the helicopter entered the canyon, the noise intensified as it echoed off the canyon walls. Kit watch as the helicopter clearly marked as Border Patrol, hovered over his two friends and then landed on a flat area in front of Swifty and Thor. One man dressed all in black exited the helicopter, and he approached Swifty and Thor with his hand on his holstered handgun. He was wearing a black baseball cap and what looked to Kit like body armor.

He talked to Swifty for about five minutes, and then Kit saw Swifty point to Kit's positon high up on the south canyon wall. The Border Patrol agent followed his pointed finger and looked straight at Kit. The radio squawked, and Kit answered it. It was Swifty.

"Stand up and wave. I'm telling him where you are so they can come up and get the burros and the dope."

Kit stood up and waved his hands over his head. The black clad agent gave him a wave and retreated to the helicopter. As soon as the agent was inside and seated, the helicopter elevated and flew westward to gain altitude. Then the craft banked up and over Kit's positon. The agents waved to him as they flew over. Kit waved back.

Swifty was back on the radio. "They'll come up and get the burros by this afternoon. They were curious about what we were doing and after I explained, they seemed fine with that. They warned us about the smugglers, and said we might expect trouble as a result of our snatching their burros and cargo."

"We'll be ready," said Kit in response.

"Roger that," replied Swifty.

Swifty and Thor pushed on with their search, pausing briefly for a lunch of sandwiches and water from their packs, while Kit ate the same meal up on the canyon rim.

At five o'clock Swifty and Thor had finished their search of the canyon floor and began the climb back up to their camp.

By the time the two men had finished their climb and arrived at their camp, Kit had dinner cooking and within half an hour they were dining on steaks and fried potatoes with applesauce for dessert. They washed down their meal with plenty of hot coffee.

True to their word, the Border Patrol had shown up on horseback and picked up the burros and their cargo after questioning Kit and then giving him a receipt for the burros and their packs.

"Do we use the same rotation for night watch?" asked Thor.

"Any volunteers for first watch?" asked Kit.

"I'll take first watch," said Swifty.

The other two men nodded their agreement, and Kit said he would relieve Swifty with Thor taking the third two-hour watch.

CHAPTER FIFTEEN

THE FIRST HOUR PASSED QUICKLY and other than the occasional rabbit or deer, Swifty saw nothing of interest through his night vision binoculars. The wind was still and yet he could hear nothing nor smell anything that was out of the ordinary.

Fifteen minutes into the third hour he saw movement at the eastern end of the canyon. As he adjusted his binoculars, he saw at least ten men on foot. Five of the men were leading burros and all of them appeared to be armed with AK-47 automatic rifles.

Unlike the previous evening's group, this one was proceeding very cautiously and slowly. They were also making a good deal of noise which had not been the case the night before.

As Swifty watched, the group stopped advancing about three hundred and fifty yards from the grove of Arizona Sycamores where the previous night's ambush had occurred.

"Why have they stopped? Are they waiting for more men? Are they waiting to see if the grove is free of any ambush?" Swifty thought to himself.

Swifty moved and nudged Kit and Thor with his boot, wakening them both silently.

Both men were quickly awake and up and had armed themselves. They joined Swifty at the observation post, and he handed Kit the binoculars. Kit looked through them and located the mysterious group. He handed the binoculars to Thor and pointed to the group's location. Thor quickly located the group and handed the binoculars back to Swifty.

"What's the plan?" Kit whispered to Swifty.

"They seem to be suspicious of the grove of trees where we were last night. I say we get down to the canyon floor, and we flank them from the south side of the canyon and surprise them."

"What if they begin moving again?," whispered Thor.

"We'll be moving toward them on their left flank and if they move, they'll be moving toward us. We spring our surprise when we are on their flank, whenever that happens," answered Swifty.

"Works for me," whispered Kit and Thor nodded his agreement.

"Let's do a weapons check before we start down," whispered Swifty.

All three men checked their weapons and then placed them all on safe.

Twenty minutes later, the three men reached the canyon floor and were making their way west along the base of the south wall of the canyon. When they reached the canyon floor, Swifty used his night vision binoculars to check on the smuggler's positon and it had not changed. He could see some of them were drinking something in cups and others were smoking cigarettes, their glow standing out like lighthouses in the dark of the canyon night.

Moving as quietly and carefully as possible they made their way along the canyon wall until they were on the smuggler's left flank. Small to large boulders and patches of mesquite provided cover between them and the smugglers.

Swifty had prepared a little surprise for the smugglers. He planned to again use his M-4 to get the smuggler's attention, but this time he had loaded his magazine with tracer bullets. When he stepped forward from behind a mesquite bush and fired a three shot burst over the heads of the smugglers, it had a dramatic effect. The tracer rounds turned the dark desert night into the Fourth of July for the ten smugglers and scared the hell out of the burros, three of whom broke their tethers and began running for the east end of the canyon.

Then the silence of the night was again broken by the loud voice of Thor yelling in Spanish for the group to surrender and throw down their guns or be killed where they stood.

Amazingly all ten of the men threw down their guns and threw their hands in the air in surrender.

Swifty and Thor moved forward to pick up the men's weapons, while Kit kept them covered.

Suddenly the night exploded in gunfire as rounds began to impact on the rocks and ground around the three Americans. Swifty and Thor hit the ground, and Kit ducked behind a large boulder. The ten smugglers remained on the ground where they had taken cover just before the firing began.

Swifty saw gun flashes from the east and from the north side of the canyon. He estimated that there were at least ten more men shooting at them.

Fortunately for the three Americans, the ambushers did not have night vision sights and most of the rounds were high and wide of their intended targets. At least two rounds did hit flesh, but both of them were on two of the unfortunate prone smugglers who were in the line of fire.

Kit concentrated his fire on the ambushers to the east of his positon. He fired and then moved to the other side of the boulder to fire again, making sure not to give the ambushers a fixed target.

Swifty concentrated his fire on the shooters to the north, while Thor found himself in a position where he had no clear shots because he had the prone smugglers directly in front of him.

Swifty reloaded his M-4 and thought to himself that he should have known that it was a set-up. It had been too easy and the smugglers had given up without any kind of resistance. The Border Patrolman's warning had been correct.

"This doesn't look good," thought Kit. "We're outnumbered and flanked and we have at least eight more of these assholes right in front of us that will jump us as soon as they think they're in control."

Swifty was worried about running out of ammunition. He had switched to single shot and was trying to make every shot count.

One of the prone smugglers was trying to crawl forward to get to his AK-47 when Thor saw him and shot the man through the knee. The wounded man began screaming in pain. Thor let the rest know in Spanish that he had plenty of rounds left for the next stupid hero. Then he moved to his right and found a good positon behind a small boulder. He began to take selected shots at the muzzle flashes of the ambushers to the east.

Suddenly there was a short burst of gunfire from the ambushers to the north and then a lot of screaming and suddenly it was deathly quiet.

Almost at once the firing from the east subsided and finally came to a halt.

Swifty was puzzled. "What's going on?," he thought.

He pulled out his night vision binoculars and scanned the area to the north where the firing and noise had come. He could see nothing, but what appeared to be several motionless prone dark figures. Then he turned his view to the east. He could make out at least six men running to the east as fast as they could. The ambush was over, but why? What had happened to the ambushers to the north?

Swifty rose from his positon and joined Thor and Kit standing over the still prone smugglers. A quick check revealed that two of the smugglers had been slightly wounded by their own ambushers and one was wounded by Thor. The burros had miraculously avoided getting shot, and all five of them had run off into the night during the gunfight.

Thor addressed the remaining ten smugglers after they had been searched for weapons and sent them back to Mexico carrying their wounded comrades. This time the smugglers were allowed to keep their clothes and boots, but not their weapons. They were given the same admonishment by Thor, "Don't come back."

With Thor providing cover, Kit and Swifty slowly advanced toward the last known position of the ambushers to the north. They moved slowly in the dark and stayed a minimum of twenty yards apart with their rifles set on fire and held at the ready positon.

"No lights," whispered Kit to the others. Kit was afraid of another ambush, and revealing their positon until they knew exactly what was what made no sense to him.

The trio spread out, as they moved slowly across the canyon floor. Each man was careful to avoid making any unnecessary noise and took care where each boot hit the hard packed floor of the canyon.

The longer they were exposed to the total darkness of the canyon, the more their night vision returned and they were able to see dim outlines in the gloom.

Swifty raised his right hand for the signal to stop and all of them froze where they were. All three men paused to sniff the air and to listen for any abnormal sounds. Satisfied that he could detect nothing that represented any danger, Swifty took his hand down and the three men continued slowly forward.

Finally, they reached the positon where the ambush had originated. Two black clad figures lay sprawled on the ground in front of them. Swifty pushed one of them with the toe of his boot and nothing happened. Then he took out a small LED flashlight and scanned the two bodies in front of him. Both bodies appeared to have been shot in the back of the head.

"Use your lights, but stay put," said Swifty.

With the three small, but powerful LED flashlights on, it did not take long for them to sweep the area and get a good idea of what lay in front of them.

There were six black clad bodies sprawled on the canyon floor in a rough semi-circle. They appeared to have been facing the position where Kit, Swifty, and Thor had been ambushed, but all six had wounds on the back of their heads.

"That one over there looks like he got hit in the head with an axe," said Thor as he began to step forward.

"Don't move, Thor," said Swifty. "This looks like a crime scene to me, and we don't want to disturb anything that the Border Patrol might see as evidence. I also don't want to give that Deputy Vegas any reason to be pissed at us."

"Swifty's right," said Kit. "As of this moment we are the likely suspects for the deaths of these guys. The Border Patrol is coming tomorrow to get the burros and the dope, and we aren't going to make them happy when we show them this mess."

"But we didn't kill them," said Thor.

"Really. So who did?" asked Swifty.

"Swifty's right. We need to stay here and wait for the Border Patrol. You two guard the site, and I'll go back to camp and use the satellite phone and call them now. The sooner this is in their hands, the better. Are you two all right with that?" asked Kit.

Both men nodded their agreement and Kit took off for the camp while Swifty and Thor found some rocks nearby to use for backrests.

"How about a fire to warm things up?" asked Thor.

"No dice. We have no idea if there are more bad guys out there in the dark, and we don't know who did this or if they might decide to take us on as well. Keep alert and your rifle at the ready."

"You're right."

The two men adjusted their positons so they sat opposite each other, and they maintained their silence as they waited for the sun to come up or Kit to return, whichever came first.

CHAPTER SIXTEEN

KIT ARRIVED BEFORE THE SUN.
"The Border Patrol is on their way and should be here by sun-up," he said.

Kit had stopped to make a thermos of coffee and some sandwiches, which he shared with Swifty and Thor. The three men hungrily wolfed down the sandwiches and drank their coffee, thankful that it was hot and strong.

About half an hour after dawn broke, they heard the sounds of an approaching helicopter. They were surprised to see two helicopters swoop down into the canyon. The copters took a pass over the canyon floor and then turned and came back and landed on level spots that were about seventy yards from where the trio waited.

Six black clad agents alighted from the helicopters. Four of them toted M-16 rifles and the other two had pistols in assault style holsters on their legs. All wore black ball caps with the border patrol insignia.

The six agents trotted over to where the three men awaited them. A barrel chested, hard featured agent with captain's bars on his black shirt stepped forward.

"Which one of you is Andrews?"

Kit raised his right hand and said, "Me, sir."

"You and your friends leave your weapons on the ground. Then move over to the copters. Sargent Bates is over there, and he'll take your statements on what happened here. But before you go, I want to make sure I got your report by phone correctly."

The captain went on to give a short hand version of what had happened that night based on what Kit had reported on the satellite phone.

"Is that basically your story?"

"Yes, sir," said all three men almost in unison.

After placing their pistols on the ground beside their rifles the trio walked over to the parked helicopters and introduced themselves to Sargent Bates. Bates directed Thor and Swifty to two other nearby agents. The three were separated by the agents and moved to different locations to give their statements to the agents.

The question and answer portion took over an hour. When they were finished, they were instructed to wait by the helicopters where they found spots on the canyon floor to sit and wait to see what would happen next.

From where they sat they could see that a yellow crime scene tape now encircled the area where the six bodies lay.

Another circle of yellow tape surrounded the spot where the trio had stood their ground during the ambush and where the original group of smugglers had been captured.

Two more hours passed and agents went back and forth from the two crime scenes and the helicopters with various items that looked like tool boxes and bags.

Finally the captain returned to where the helicopters were parked.

After he had talked with Sargent Bates and read the statements that each of the three men had given, he walked over to them.

"I'm Captain Vonalt and I have a few more questions for you three. I've seen some crazy things out here on the border and some pretty bad things as well, but this one is a first."

"What do you mean, Captain?" asked Kit.

The captain lowered himself to the ground where he sat at the same level as the trio. He took off his hat and wiped the sweat from his forehead. He rubbed the hat band with his hand and then replaced it on his head. Then he looked straight at Kit.

"According to your statements you men are all from Wyoming, and you are here at the request of a relative to try to locate a missing man. You got involved in trying to stop a group smuggling drugs into the U.S., and then got ambushed by parties unknown. Is that correct?"

"Yes sir, that is correct," said Kit.

"My first impression was that you were a bunch of vigilantes who killed a group of Mexican nationals in a gun fight. If so, I would have to arrest you and confiscate your weapons as evidence."

All three men looked at the captain in surprise.

"But, our examination of the crime scene rules that out."

"What did you find?" asked Kit.

Captain Vonalt paused before he answered Kit. He pulled at the corner of his moustache and then looked up at the three men.

"In my twenty years in the Border Patrol I have seen all kinds of killings. I've seen men, women, and children murdered in unbelievably horrible ways. But I have never seen men killed this way."

"What way?" asked all three men in unison.

"All six of the Mexican national victims were killed by what appears to be edged weapon blows to the head and neck. None of the victims were killed by a bullet wound. None of you have hatchets, axes, or tomahawks on your person or in your camp. I believe you had nothing to do with the deaths of the six Mexican nationals, but I have no clues as to who did kill them or why."

The three men sat in stunned silence.

Kit was the first to speak. "Are we free to go?"

"I have no reason to hold you. I appreciate your assistance in retrieving the burros loaded with drugs, but I have to advise you that staying in this canyon is not a good idea. You have already seen what can happen here, especially at night. I can't even get volunteers from my own agents to come in here at night unless there are at least six of them. I'd advise you to abandon your search and leave this canyon. To my knowledge nothing good has ever happened here, and last night only adds to that opinion."

"I understand your positon, Captain Vonalt, but we took on a job and it's not finished. We are capable of taking care of ourselves, and we intend to stay until we find Leon Turner or what's left of him so we can give his family some answers."

"I hear you, Mr. Andrews. Just be aware that while I may personally admire what you are trying to do, I professionally have to advise you to leave. Off the record, I am not sorry to see those six Mexicans dead. We have identified all of them as cartel members, who are on our wanted posters for crimes in the U.S. However, now I have a new problem of trying to find out who killed them and why. If they'll kill Mexicans, who is to say they won't kill Americans as well. It appears to me that you boys pissed off a cartel when you captured that dope shipment, and they sent out a second group of smugglers as bait so they could ambush you and wipe you out. Something else happened that had nothing to do with you or the cartel, and I'm at a loss as how to explain it. Whatever it was, you boys were lucky. I wouldn't press my luck if I were you."

"I understand, Captain Vonalt," said Kit.

"I'm going to leave four men here, and we'll have a larger helicopter here within a couple of hours to pick up the bodies. After that, you're on your own. You can retrieve your weapons from Agent Gonzales. He's one of the four men guarding the crime scene. Good luck and good hunting, gentlemen."

"Thank you, Captain," said Kit.

The captain rose to his feet as did each of the three men. He walked to the waiting helicopter and stopped before he entered it. He turned and gave the three men a salute by touching the brim of his cap. He grinned at them and swung into the copter and was no sooner seated when the copter lifted off. Within minutes both of the helicopters had vanished from sight with only the echo of their engines and rotors as evidence that they had ever been in the canyon.

"Let's go get our stuff," said Kit.

The three men rose and headed for the yellow tape marked crime scene and the remaining four Border Patrol agents.

As they neared the crime scene, one of the four agents moved toward them with his left hand up and his right hand resting on the butt of his holstered pistol.

"You men stop right there. This is a crime scene."

"The captain told us to come over and retrieve our weapons," said Kit.

The agent gave them a hard look and then said, "Follow me over here."

The agent led them to a small tarp spread out over the hard ground. On the tarp were all of their rifles and pistols.

"Just sign this receipt, and you're welcome to your weapons," said the agent as he held out a clipboard with a pen attached.

All three men signed the receipt, and then took possession of their weapons. The agent stood quietly by and watched them pick-up and check their weapons.

"That's all of them?" asked the agent.

"Yes sir, it is," said Kit.

"Can I ask a question?" said Swifty.

"Go ahead," said the agent.

Swifty had noticed that the nametag on the agent's uniform said "Brody."

"Agent Brody, would it be all permissible if I could get a look at the wounds on one of the bodies?"

"I think I can allow that, just don't touch the body and only walk where I tell you," replied Brody.

Swifty followed agent Brody under the yellow tape and over to where the bodies were located. All six of the corpses were encased in black plastic body bags. Agent Brody knelt by the first bag and unzipped it about three feet which exposed the head and upper torso of the dead Mexican.

Without moving the body it was apparent to Swifty that the wound was made by a hatchet or axe head. The result was gruesome and bloody. Swifty stood up and faced Brody.

"Thank you for letting me take a look, Agent Brody."

"Pretty ugly way to die," said Brody.

"It wouldn't be my choice."

"It wouldn't be mine either."

"There is one more thing, Agent Brody."

"What's that?"

"Do you mind if I look around outside the crime scene tape?"

"Knock yourself out. Just let me know if you see something we might have missed."

"I'll be happy to, and thank you," said Swifty.

Swifty returned to where Kit and Thor stood and told them he was going to take a look around and told them to get comfortable and wait for him.

"Don't you want us to help?" asked Thor.

Swifty just grinned at him and handed his rifle to Kit and began to move slowly in half circles around the northern half of the crime scene. After he completed a half circle, Swifty began a new one about four yards further out.

Both Kit and Thor knew that Swifty was looking for signs that might lend a clue as to who the killers were.

Swifty had been slowly moving in half circles to the north of the crime scene for over an hour when another Border Patrol helicopter arrived. It was larger than the others Kit had seen. He looked over at Thor.

"It's an old Huey like the kind they used in Vietnam," said Thor in answer to the unasked question.

The helicopter landed and disgorged three crime scene technicians, who promptly began to photograph the crime scene and carefully search it from one end to the other.

While Kit and Thor were watching the technicians work, Swifty silently appeared at their side. All three men remained in place for another two hours until the Border Patrol technicians were finished. The agents were loading the body bags into the Huey and the technicians were pacing up their gear when Swifty rose to his feet and approached Agent Brody.

"Did the killers take anything?" he asked Brody.

Brody thought for a moment and then spoke. "All of the weapons, ammo and gear were missing."

"How about wallets and money?"

"They weren't touched,"

"Thanks, Agent Brody."

"No problem," said Brody, and he headed for the waiting Huey.

A few minutes later, the Huey lifted off with its grisly cargo.

When the Huey and its attendant noise had disappeared from sight and sound, Swifty rose to his feet. He quickly walked to a spot about forty yards north of the still present yellow crime scene tape and stopped at a spot behind a small boulder. He took his cell phone out of his pocket and after making an adjustment, he used the camera mode to take a couple of photos. He checked the phone to review the photos, and then he shut the cell off and put it back in his pocket.

Kit and Thor had collected their weapons and were waiting for Swifty under the meager shade of an Arizona Sycamore. Swifty walked over and joined the duo by sitting on a rock under the tree.

"Well, what did you find out?" asked Kit.

"I have no doubt that all six of those dudes were killed with one or two strokes of a hatchet or a tomahawk."

"How could all six of them have been killed by tomahawks at the same time? Those guys were armed with AK-47s."

"Actually, it was pretty easy. The six Mexicans were facing us and concentrating on their ambush. The noise of the rifles drowned out any noise that might have alerted them. Six or more intruders slipped in behind the shooters and at a signal, they all stepped forward and each killed the man in front of him with a tomahawk blow to the head."

"Why are you so sure the weapons were tomahawks and not hatchets?"

"I'm sure because of what I found up in the rocks to the north of the bodies."

"What did you find?"

Swifty took out his smart phone and hit a couple of buttons and showed the resulting photograph to Kit and Thor.

"What's that?" asked Thor.

"That, my friends, is a picture of a moccasin print in one of the few areas of soft dirt in those rocks behind where the bodies were."

"A moccasin print!"

"That's what I said, Thor, a moccasin print, and a fresh one to boot."

"Who would be wearing moccasins up in this rugged country?" asked Kit.

"When we figure that out, we'll know who killed these six dudes."

CHAPTER SEVENTEEN

KIT LED THE WAY AS the three men made their way back up the narrow trail from the canyon floor to the south rim, where there camp was located.

Kit and Swifty went over all of the weapons and carefully cleaned the rifles while Thor busied himself making a quick lunch of sandwiches and coffee.

"We were lucky," said Swifty.

"You mean with getting the unexpected help in ruining the cartel's ambush?"

"No, not the ambush. I mean that when the Border Patrol checked our weapons, they missed the fact that mine is an M-4 and yours are AR-15s.

"I'm not sure I follow what you mean," said Kit.

"My M-4 is capable of an automatic three shot burst and your AR-15s are semi-automatic with only one shot at a time. The M-4 is technically illegal as it is in effect a sub-machine gun, and something we're not supposed to have."

"That's a joke considering that all of those Mexican dudes had AK-47s that are fully automatic."

"Their guns are illegal, but as you can see it didn't seem to bother them at all when they were shooting at us last night."

"The AK-47s didn't do them a lot of good against something as primitive as a tomahawk," said Kit.

"Most of the time automatic weapons don't actually give the shooter the advantage they should," said Swifty.

"Why is that?"

"For one thing the recoil from an automatic weapon forces the muzzle of the gun up. For another it encourages a method known in the military as spray and pray. Most AK-47 shooters become overly impressed with their firepower and forget the need to aim and make each shot count."

Thor interrupted their conversation with a yell that lunch was ready, and both men joined Thor in the relative shade of the cave.

After they had finished lunch, Swifty poured himself another cup of coffee. After seating himself on the floor of the cave next to Kit and Thor, he took a sip of his hot coffee and looked up at the two men.

"I've been thinking about this search we're on. We have finished a basic search of the canyon floor, but we haven't even begun looking at the two side canyons or all of the gullies and arroyos that make up the edges and walls of the main canyon. At this rate we could be here for a month."

"So what are you suggesting?" asked Kit.

"We need reinforcements and some professional help. I think we need to call Big Dave and tell him what we have found and see what he suggests."

"That makes perfect sense to me," said Kit. "I was wondering how we were going to search above the canyon floor."

Kit broke out the satellite phone and after a few adjustments to the instrument and waiting for satellite connections, he finally got a dial tone and called Big Dave's phone number. Big Dave did not answer, so Kit left a detailed message along with the number of his satellite phone and hung up.

"Big Dave didn't answer, so I left a message. I suggest we take a nap while we wait for him to return the call. I'll take first watch."

"That works for me," said Thor, and Swifty nodded and grinned in agreement.

Twenty minutes later the quiet of the desert was broken by two sets of loud snoring.

Kit made a fresh pot of coffee and then poured himself a cup. He made himself as comfortable as possible in the look-out positon and realized it would be difficult to fall asleep on watch with all the loud snoring of his companions.

The afternoon passed quickly and when his two hours was up, Kit decided to let the others sleep and he stayed on watch until the sun was about to go down below the horizon. He had seen nothing on the canyon floor, with the exception of a couple of coyotes looking for their supper.

Kit used his boot toe to nudge Thor and Swifty awake. Both men were quickly up and dressed and pulling on their boots.

"Don't forget to shake your boots out to make sure no scorpion has decided to become a nester," said Kit.

Both Thor and Swifty carefully shook their boots, and Swifty went further and pounded his upside down boots on a nearby rock.

"Can't be too careful when it comes to those nasty little critters," said Swifty.

Thor looked up at the setting sun and said, "I'll rustle up some supper."

"I'll give you a hand," said Kit. Kit made his way to the supply pack on the floor of the cave when he was interrupted by the ringing of his satellite phone. He pulled the phone out of his pocket and pushed the button to answer the incoming call.

"Hello to you, Big Dave. I assume you got my message. Yeah, we're all fine. You want to do what? Yeah, we can do that. When will you be here? Yes, we can meet you at the trailhead north of Douglas by where we parked our truck and trailer. We'll bring the mules for resupply and leave one of us behind to guard the camp. Give me a call when you are about thirty miles out of Douglas and that should give us time to get to the truck and meet you. All right, we'll see you in two days. Take care. Bye."

"So what's the deal?" asked Swifty.

"Big Dave's got a plan to search the canyon. He wants us to search the side canyons and nearby arroyos during the next two days and then meet him with the mules at the truck. He'll call when he's about thirty miles, out of Douglas and that should give us time to get to the truck with the mules. He'll resupply us with water and food and then fill us in on his plan."

"Is he bringing more manpower?"

"It sounded like it. He's bringing more pack animals and some high tech help is what he said."

"High tech help for Big Dave is liable to be something with batteries," said Swifty.

"Maybe he's bringing us a hot air balloon," laughed Thor.

"Whatever he's bringing us is more than we have, and Lord knows we can use some help," said Kit.

"Speaking of help, grab some supplies so I can get on with fixin' supper," said Thor.

"What's on the menu tonight, Chef Thor?" chortled Swifty.

"I ain't sure about you boys, but I'm in the mood for flapjacks and bacon and eggs."

"I want what the chef wants," said Kit.

Thor and Kit gathered what supplies they would need and Thor began cooking while Kit got out paper plates and utensils.

Their supper consumed and cooking gear cleaned up and put away, the trio sat down by the lip of the canyon and drank hot coffee.

"What's the plan, Kit?" asked Swifty.

"We keep watch tonight, and tomorrow we start searching the side canyons."

Kit pulled a topographical map out of his vest pocket and spread it on the ground in front of him. He pointed to the two side canyons on the south side of Skeleton Canyon.

"Tomorrow Swifty and I will search Pony Canyon and any side arroyos leading up to it. Thor keeps watch up at the camp. The following day Thor and I search Pine Canyon and the nearby arroyos, and Swifty keeps watch. Each day we take our lunch with us. The satellite phone stays with the guy on watch."

"What about traffic in the canyon?" asked Swifty.

"We avoid any contact unless it's the Border Patrol. Big Dave wants us to lay low and be alert for any further moves by the cartel. I agree with him. I think the cartel is probably really pissed and trying to figure out what happened last night."

"Good luck with that. We don't even know what happened last night in the canyon, and we were there," said Thor.

"We go in with side arms, and we keep to ourselves. If we see anyone, we hide out in the rocks until they're gone. Whoever is on watch, keeps us informed by radio so we don't get any unpleasant surprises," said Kit.

The early dark of evening was limiting their view of the canyon, and they decided to call it a day and get as much sleep as possible. Swifty took the watch, and Kit and Thor slipped into their sleeping bags. Fifteen minutes later Swifty was alone with the sound of his partner's snores.

Swifty made it a routine to use his night vision binoculars every ten minutes to scan both ends of the canyon floor. Because of his earlier nap he extended his watch from two hours to almost four and he still saw no movement in his scans of the canyon floor.

Kit was awakened by the toe of Swifty's boot. He quickly dressed and after shaking his boots, he put them on and joined Swifty at the look-out point.

"See anything?"

"Not a thing. Nothing has moved into the canyon for the past four hours."

"You kept on watch for four hours?"

"Hey, I had a nap. I'm fine and still not too sleepy. I thought if I stayed here and listened to you talk, I'd be asleep in no time from boredom."

"I can't help it if your brain is so small that anything over two sentences causes it to go into overload."

"My brain is selective about what it allows in, and it has a very sensitive bullshit meter, which is why listening to you is always boring."

"Your brain is limited to things you approve of like loose women, fast horses, and cheap whiskey."

"I have no argument with any of those choices."

Something caught Kit's eye, and he raised the night vision binoculars and a slow sweep of the eastern end of the canyon revealed movement.

As Kit adjusted the focus on the binoculars, he could make out movement as another group of illegals trying to enter Arizona through the canyon. He could make out what he thought were three coyotes leading a mixed group of fifteen adults and children.

"What do you see?" asked Swifty.

"It's another group of illegals coming from the east end of the canyon."

"Do we let them go?"

"We're to keep a low profile, and I'm pretty sure that means avoiding any contact or doing anything that brings the Border Patrol back with more questions."

"Well, have fun. I'm hitting the sack. Talking to you has plumb worn me out."

Kit bit off his smart-ass reply and just grinned at his partner.

"Sleep tight, you wayward hillbilly."

"Your jealousy just makes you look bad."

"I'd be jealous if there were something to be jealous of."

"A man's gotta know his limitations, and you got a lot of them partner."

"I'm comfortable with my faults, Swifty."

"Wake me when it's my watch."

Kit just grunted in reply.

Kit maintained his watch for three hours before waking Thor for his watch. Thor awoke as soon as the toe of Kit's boot touched his shoulder.

"Any more activity in the canyon?"

"Not a thing except for a couple of deer."

"See you in the morning, Kit."

Kit slipped into his sleeping bag and was soon sound asleep.

Thor changed positions several times to keep awake and alert. Despite his deliberate sweeps of the canyon with his night vision binoculars, he saw absolutely nothing. He was happy to see the sun come up.

The trio was up early the next morning and Thor quickly made a breakfast of eggs, bacon, and dehydrated hash browns which they washed down with hot coffee. After cleaning up the breakfast gear, Kit and Swifty packed a lunch and extra water. Both men carried pistols in holsters and each had added Gerber MLF sheath knives on their belts.

Their ascent down the narrow trail went quickly, as they had become accustomed to it. Kit did a radio check with Thor back at camp, and then they set out for Pony Canyon.

On their way to the entrance to Pony Canyon, Kit and Swifty carefully searched each of the arroyos they encountered that reached the canyon floor on the south side of the canyon.

Careful searches of the several arroyos they encountered revealed nothing that would suggest that any human had been there, let alone Leon Turner.

CHAPTER EIGHTEEN

FINALLY THEY REACHED THE ENTRANCE to Pony Canyon. Pony Canyon was essentially a box canyon with the only access being the entrance from Skeleton Canyon. The two men began making their way around the base of the canyon walls moving in a clockwise fashion from the entrance.

At the entrance to the fourth arroyo, Swifty came to a silent halt and held up his hand to signal Kit to stop. Both men dropped to a crouch and remained motionless and silent as they scanned the arroyo and listened carefully. They could hear movement, but they could not see anything. Swifty motioned with his hand for Kit to move to the south side of the arroyo and to remain silent. Kit moved, and both men drew their pistols and waited.

They could hear the sounds of boots on the loose rocks in the arroyo and finally they could hear the sounds of heavy breathing. Suddenly they could see two young white men making their way clumsily down the arroyo to the canyon floor. The two men were skinny and dressed in t-shirts and walking shorts while wearing baseball type caps. Each of them had a small backpack. One of them was taller and had a wispy moustache and wore glasses. Both young men looked exhausted.

Swifty looked at Kit and then holstered his pistol, and Kit did likewise. Swifty stepped into the view of the young men and waited for them to reach his position. Kit remained out of sight on the other side of the arroyo. From this positon he could provide cover for Swifty if anything went wrong.

The two young men staggered to a stop in front of Swifty. Both men leaned forward and placed their hands on their knees. They were obviously exhausted and their caps and t-shirts were soaked with sweat.

"Howdy," said Swifty. "Are you boys all right?"

The taller one with the glasses stood upright and looked at Swifty like he was trying to make sure that Swifty was real or not.

"Actually, sir, we're in a bit of trouble."

"What seems to be the problem?"

"My name is Adam and this is my friend Howard. We're birders."

"Birders?"

"We're bird watchers. We started out from the east end of Skeleton Canyon looking for a rare species of bird known as the Elegant Trogan."

"Elegant Trogan?"

"Yes. It's a bird found in Mexico that is only rarely seen in southern Arizona or southern New Mexico, and they had allegedly been sighted in Skeleton Canyon."

"Why in Skeleton Canyon?"

"They are attracted to the presence of the Arizona Sycamore tree and there are many of those trees in Skeleton Canyon."

"So what happened to you?"

"Well, we were depending on the maps stored in our smart, phone and we took some wrong turns and we got lost. We spent the night on a ridgeline and then the batteries in the smart phone died and we had no maps or compass. My Camelbac bladder developed a leak I didn't notice and we ran out of water. We've been trying to find our way back to our Subaru, but we seem to keep taking wrong turns and we have no idea where we are. You wouldn't happen to have any water to spare?"

Swifty motioned for Kit to join him and he took note that both young men looked to be more academic than athletic and both were sunburned and their lips were dry and cracked. He took out a water bottle and handed it to the one called Adam, and Kit retrieved one of his water bottles and handed it to the shorter one called Howard.

Both young men drank greedily from the water bottles.

"Don't drink so fast. Slow down and drink slowly," said Swifty.

Both Adam and Howard stopped and drinking and first Adam and then Howard sank down and sat on the hard canyon floor. They then began taking sips of water and trying to pace themselves as they drank with a relish as though they were savoring a rare wine.

Swifty and Kit went to one knee and waited for the two young men to finally slake their thirst. Finally Adam stopped drinking and handed the bottle out to Swifty.

"Keep it, Adam. You're gonna need it. You still have about a five mile walk back to where your vehicle is probably located."

Swifty took off his pack and pulled out a topographical map and laid it down on the canyon floor. He pointed to a spot on the map.

"This here is Pony Canyon and this is where we are. Right behind me is the entrance from Pony Canyon to Skeleton Canyon. You go into Skeleton Canyon and then turn left or east and follow the canyon floor until you reach the east entrance. That is about four miles from here. Your vehicle has to be somewhere east of there. You and your friend take the map and the water bottles and head out."

Adam looked at Swifty in amazement. Finally he spoke.

"What do you want for the map and the water bottles?"

"We want nothing,"

"I don't know how to thank you. You have no idea of how much this means. I thought we were going to die out here."

"You owe us nothing. You'd do the same for us."

Howard joined his friend in thanking Kit and Swifty. Finally, Swifty put up his hand to stop their blubbering.

"Next time never go into the canyons without plenty of water and a good map and a compass. Also take extra batteries for your phone. I'd also suggest buying a portable GPS, also with extra batteries."

Kit pulled off his pack and rummaged through it and came up with a tube of lip balm and a tube of aloe cream.

"Here, apply the balm to your lips and then take the tube and gently rub the aloe on your exposed skin that is sunburned," said Kit to the two young men.

Adam took the lip balm and aloe from Kit and after applying it, he passed the items on to Howard who wasted no time in applying them.

"I'm starting to feel better already," said Adam.

"You guys didn't happen to see anything unusual in your wanderings around the canyon, did you?" asked Swifty.

"We saw some birds, some lizards, and some trash we think was left by illegals."

"What kind of trash?"

"Stuff like used toilet paper, empty water bottles and candy bar wrappers."

"You saw nothing else that looked like it didn't belong there?"

"No, nothing else. What did you think we saw?"

"We're looking for a missing man, and I thought you might have seen some camping gear, some clothing, boots, or some bones."

Adam looked at Swifty in horror.

"You're asking if we saw a body."

"We don't know if the man we're looking for is dead or alive, but we are presuming the worst."

"We saw nothing like that."

"You two had better head on back to your vehicle. We need to get back to our search."

Both young men struggled to their feet. "We'll remember your advice, and we sincerely thank you both," said Adam.

Swifty and Kit shook hands with the two birders and watched as they made their way out of Pony Canyon and turned to the east in Skeleton Canyon.

"You think they'll make it?" asked Kit.

"If they can remember where they left their vehicle when they get to the New Mexico end of the canyon, they'll be fine. If not, I have no idea."

"You don't think there is any chance they might be working for the cartel and being used to find us?"

"I got no indication that they were interested in anything but drinking water and finding a way out of here."

"Let's get back to work," said Kit.

Swifty and Kit resumed their search and spent a great deal of time climbing up the arroyos to the top and moving laterally to the next arroyo and then climbing down to the canyon floor.

After about four hours they had completed their circuit of the arroyos that slashed down from the canyon walls to the floor of Pony Canyon. They took a break under the sparse shade of a large growth of Mesquite bushes and ate their sandwiches washed down with water. Both men's clothes were soaked with sweat and stained with salt from their physical exertions in the hot sun.

After a half hour break, they resumed their search of the canyon floor covering it in grid search where they walked parallel with a distance of ten yards between them. Three hours later they had found nothing that would suggest a link to the lost Leon Turner.

They finished their search of Pony Canyon and stopped by the entrance to Skeleton Canyon, sitting in the late afternoon shade of the west wall of Pony Canyon. Kit was exhausted and glad for the slight coolness of the shade the canyon wall afforded them. He closed his eyes and stretched his legs and back to try to get the stiffness out of them.

When Kit opened his eyes, he could see Swifty sitting up with his back to the canyon wall. Swifty's head was on a swivel as he slowly scanned the walls of Pony Canyon with his eyes.

"Do you see something out there?" he asked Swifty.

"It isn't what I see, it's what I feel."

Kit came to full alert and used his eyes to scan the canyon. He closed his eyes and listened. He could hear nothing but his and Swifty's breathing. He sniffed the air and he could smell nothing different that seemed out of place.

"What is it that you feel?"

"I feel like we're being watched."

"Watched by whom?"

"I have no idea and like I said, I've not seen, heard, nor smelled anything wrong. But I have this feeling that there is something out there that's been watching us for the past two hours."

"You don't think it was those two young birders?"

"Not a chance in hell it was those two. They were zoned in on getting to their vehicle and getting the hell out of Skeleton Canyon. Those two were stupid and exhausted, not devious. Nobody could act that well and fake being that physically exhausted and sunburned."

"Do you think we are talking about some dudes from the cartel?"

"I don't know who they are or even if they're humans, but I can't shake this feeling and it's never been wrong before."

"So what do we do?"

"We head back to the camp, and we stop every now and then and use our senses to see if we're being followed."

"Sounds like a plan to me. Let's move out."

The two men rose to their feet and after adjusting their gear, started to walk out of Pony Canyon. At the entrance to Skeleton Canyon Kit pulled out his radio and hit the transmit button to call Thor.

Thor answered almost immediately.

"How are you two doing down there. I was getting worried that I hadn't heard from you."

"We're fine, and we've finished up on our search of Pony Canyon," said Kit.

"Did you find anything in the canyon?"

"Just a couple of lost bird watchers. We sent them to the east end of the canyon to find their vehicle. Did you see them move through the canyon?"

"I saw two dorks stumbling along and heading east to the New Mexico entrance several hours ago."

"Did they make it to the east end of the canyon?"

"When they moved out of my vision, they were still walking east and they seemed all right, but they were stumbling like they were really tired."

"That doesn't surprise me. They were bushed when we found them."

"Did you find anything else?"

"We found nothing else. Did you see anything else going on in the canyon or up on the canyon walls?"

"I've seen some birds, some coyotes, and a few rabbits and lizards."

"You've seen nothing that looked like some of our friends from the south?"

"I've seen nothing that was remotely human, if that's what you're asking."

"We're headed in and should be there in about an hour and a half."

"Me and the mules will be waitin'."

Kit replaced the radio in his pack, and he and Swifty began their walk through the canyon to the base of the trail that led up the canyon wall to their camp.

CHAPTER NINETEEN

BOTH SWIFTY AND KIT WERE bone tired when they finally reached camp. Thor produced two water bottles he had kept in the shade of the cave to keep them cool. Both men sucked down the water greedily and then lay back on the hard, but cool rocks in the floor of the cave.

In ten minutes they were fast asleep. Thor grinned to himself as he made himself busy preparing supper. After he had finished cooking and taken time to water and feed the mules, he awakened his companions by banging two skillets together. Both Kit and Swifty jumped to their feet in alarm to the roaring laughter of Thor.

"What the hell is the alarm all about?" grumbled Swifty.

"Supper's ready and if you ain't, then I plan to eat it all myself," replied Thor.

Both Kit and Swifty had to smile and their mood changed quickly when they smelled the aroma of Thor's cooking efforts.

"What's for supper?" asked Kit.

"Beef! That's what for supper. What did you expect? We don't serve no tofu," bellowed Thor.

Supper was a thick and savory beef stew with thick slices of bread covered with butter. Supper was excellent, and the beef stew was washed down with cans of beer kept cool in the back of the cave. After eating the beef stew, the men used the thick slices of bread to sop up all the gravy and stew remains on their plates.

Kit and Swifty cleaned up the supper dishes and afterward the three men sat by the edge of the top of the canyon wall.

Swifty broke out three fine cigars, a lighter, and his pocket knife. After cutting off the end of the cigar with the knife, he lit it with the lighter and passed the lighter, cigars, and knife on to the other two men.

As the sunlight faded and darkness descended on their camp, the air was filled with the fragrant smoke of the cigars. Kit produced a small bottle of excellent eight year old bourbon and three tin cups. By the time the moon was visible in the night sky, all that could be seen of the trio's camp was the soft glow of three cigars in the darkness.

"This is one hell of a good cigar. Where'd you get these cigars, Swifty?" asked Thor.

"It's better that you don't know," replied Swifty.

"What do you mean by that?"

"Let's just say I got them from a friend of a friend of a friend who spends time traveling to and from Cuba."

"So these cigars are illegal?"

"You could say that."

"No wonder they taste so good. Illegal always makes them better."

All three men broke out in laughter.

Their cigars finished, Kit and Swifty headed for their sleeping bags and Thor made himself comfortable in the look-out positon and began searching the canyon with the night vision binoculars.

Morning found Swifty cooking a hot breakfast of bacon and eggs along with a pot of fresh coffee. As the three men ate, they exchanged information from their watches of the previous night. Other than one group of illegals, none of them had seen anything unusual.

"Well, there was one thing," said Thor.

"You saw something last night?" asked Kit.

"It wasn't something I saw."

"So you heard something?" asked Kit.

"No. It wasn't anything I heard."

"Let me guess. You smelled something," joked Swifty.

"Nope. It was something I felt."

"What do you mean something you felt? Did something touch you?"

"Nothing touched me. I just felt like I was being watched. I felt it several time during the first hour of my watch. Then the feeling went away and I didn't feel it again."

Swifty and Kit looked at each other.

"You two clean up the breakfast dishes, and I think I'll take a look around," said Swifty.

Swifty began doing half circle searches around their camp. Each time he finished a circle, he reversed himself and followed a new circle about five yards further out from the camp.

Kit and Thor had finished cleaning up the camp, and they had assembled their gear for the day's search when Swifty returned to the cave.

"Find anything?" asked Kit.

"Just this," said Swifty as he pulled out his cell phone and pressed a couple of buttons until a photo came into view.

"That's that moccasin print you found yesterday by the crime scene," said Thor.

"No, it's not. This is a photo I just took about eighty yards to the west of our camp."

None of the three men said a thing. They just stood, staring at the photo on Swifty's cell phone.

"Holy shit! This is getting a little too spooky for me," said Thor.

"It means your senses were on alert last night, and your senses were right. Something was out there, and that something was wearing moccasins."

Kit looked all around the edges of the camp and then said, "You keep alert, Swifty. We will too. Anything feels wrong, give us a call and we'll come running."

"You boys have a good search of Pine Canyon, and I'll see if I can learn anything more about our night visitor."

Kit and Thor headed down the trail and as soon as they were out of sight, Swifty pulled out his M-4 and put a fresh magazine of ammo in it.

Thor had stopped to take a drink from his water bottle when both he and Kit heard a familiar noise.

Both men's heads snapped up and their hands went to their side arms. They moved quickly to the side of some large rocks and a stand of mesquite bushes for cover.

The noise of a truck or auto engine coming from the west end of the canyon was getting louder and they could see a broom-tail of dust rising above the brush on the horizon to the west.

As they waited behind the rocks, the noise grew louder and finally an old CJ-7 Jeep roared into view as it made its way expertly around the trees and rocks that littered the floor of the canyon.

Just as the Jeep neared their hiding positon, it came to a halt and the motor was turned off. A large white man wearing sunglasses, a straw cowboy hat and dressed in jeans and a denim cowboy shirt jumped out of the driver's seat. Scuffed up cowboy boots completed his rig.

The man was about six foot three in height and he was built like a blacksmith. He walked around the Jeep and faced the rocks they were hiding behind.

"You boys can come out. I was watching you walking from about half a mile away with my binoculars."

Kit looked out at the man. He was not carrying any weapons that Kit could see, although he did see what looked like a Winchester Model 94 lever action rifle in a scabbard strapped to the roll bar of the Jeep. Kit's radio buzzed. Swifty called to find out who the intruder in the Jeep was.

"Hang tight, Swifty. I'll call you back."

Kit and Thor stepped from behind the rocks to meet this mysterious newcomer.

The man extended his hand to Kit and introduced himself. "Howdy. I'm Buck Slaughter. I'm the manager of the Sloan Ranch."

"I'm Kit Andrews and this here is Thor Olson. I was trying to figure out how you got a vehicle into the canyon, and I assume it's because it's your ranch that's between the canyon and Highway 80."

"You figure right. I heard on my scanner about the Border Patrol being in the canyon investigating some dustup that got some cartel boys shot up and others sent scampering for the border. I fired up old Nellie here and headed out to see what was goin' on in the canyon. Are you the fellas who were involved?"

"That would be us," replied Kit.

"So what really happened? I know what the Border Patrol puts out has been run through some washing machine about eight times and any relation to reality is an accident on their part."

Kit and Thor looked at each other and both grinned. This was their kind of cowboy.

Kit proceeded to tell Buck what had happened and explained why they were in the canyon in the first place.

"You know talking this much is kind of out of character for me. I avoid it because it makes my throat get dry and in this country that's a bad idea. Would you two like to join me in a cold beer to wash down the dust?"

"Absolutely," said Thor. Kit just smiled.

Ten minutes later the three men were sitting in the temporary shade of a large boulder drinking cold cans of Bud Lite that Buck had produced from a cooler in the back of his Jeep.

"So why did you decide to close the gate on the county road into Skeleton Canyon?"

"We got tired of a parade of illegals and dope smugglers running through the canyon and across our ranch land. Those bastards cut fences, shot cows, and left piles of garbage all over the ranch. We appealed to the county, the state and the feds, and we got no help. So we decided to make it harder to get through by closing and locking the road gate. We kind of hoped that people would get pissed and complain, and then we might get some action from the law."

"So what happened?"

"We got plenty of people pissed at us, especially the hunters in the fall, but the county did nothing but talk about it and nothing changed."

"We've seen plenty of illegals led by coyotes coming through the canyon as well as the drug smugglers over the past two days," said Thor.

"This canyon has been a highway from Mexico for over a hundred years. The Apache were the historic users and now it's the illegals and dope smugglers. I came out here to see what was going on. After I heard about the dustup and the fact that some cowboys were involved, I wanted to meet them and shake their hand. I can't begin to tell you how sick I am of cleaning up after those Mexican bastards."

"Have you ever tried to do anything to disrupt the traffic in the canyon?" asked Thor.

"I got a three man crew running a ranch that has several thousand acres. Add to that cleaning up after the Mexicans and I ain't got time to take a shit, let alone spend my nights setting up ambushes in the canyon. If I did anything, I run the risk of getting in trouble with the Border Patrol and the county. Now I ain't sayin' that I ain't never done nothing like that, but let's just say for the rest of the world, nothing like that has ever happened. You savvy?"

"Your last name sounds familiar," said Kit. "Are you in any way related to the legendary John H. Slaughter, owner of the Slaughter Ranch?"

"I am proud to admit I am a distant kin of old John Slaughter."

Buck was obviously pleased Kit had known about John H. Slaughter and the Slaughter Ranch, and it showed by the smile on his face and in his twinkling light blue eyes.

"The Slaughter Ranch was located south of here?"

"Yup. The ranch is just this side of the Mexican border to the east of Douglas. It's a National Historic Site now. I think old John Slaughter would roll over in his grave if he could see what's going on in Cochise County today."

"If I recall correctly, John Slaughter was a Texan who cleaned up the rustling and crooks from Cochise County and he ran crooks out of Tombstone as well."

"You heard right. Old John used to look a crook in the eye and tell him to get out of town or John would kill them. Worked wonders for cleaning up crime," said Buck with a wide grin.

"I'm assuming you know Skeleton Canyon as well as anyone, Buck," said Kit.

"I been working for the Sloan Ranch for fifteen years, and I probably been in this canyon a hundred times. I don't claim to know every nook and cranny, but I know most of it pretty well."

"In your hundred plus trips to Skeleton Canyon, have you ever seen or heard anything unusual?"

"You'd have to explain what you mean by unusual. I've seen all kinds of things that are usually the result of man tangling with this canyon, and man is usually the loser."

"I told you that six of the cartel dudes were killed, but I didn't tell you how."

"What do you mean by how they were killed?"

"I mean they were killed by blows by edged weapons to the back of the head."

"You mean like with an axe?"

"We think it was by use of a tomahawk."

"A tomahawk? You're kidding, right?"

"I'm not kidding, and our partner Swifty found a moccasin print in some soft earth from the area where the killers came."

"A moccasin print? I hate to say it, Kit, but you sound like you been out in the sun too long. In all the time I've spent in this canyon, I never seen a moccasin print. I've seen boot prints and prints made by bare feet, not to mention horseshoe prints, but that's been it."

"How about this. Have you ever felt like you were being watched when you were in the canyon?"

"Watched by whom?"

"I have no idea. I just want to know if you've ever had that feeling."

"Well, I'd be a liar if I said I never felt edgy when I was in this canyon alone. Too many bad things have happened in Skeleton Canyon over the years. Lots of folks have died and none in a nice way. I have had the hair on the back of my neck stand up, and I couldn't explain why. I always felt like I was feeling the presence of the dead. It felt like I was feeling the presence of the ghosts of Skeleton Canyon."

"So you felt something, but you never actually saw anything?"

"I'd say that was pretty accurate. I never saw anything that wasn't supposed to be in the canyon. Are you saying you've seen something here?"

"No, I am not saying that at all. I've just felt like there was someone or something watching me at times. Like you, I've never seen anything to support that feeling.

"This place does give me the willies," said Thor.

By now Buck had made two trips to the Jeep and the three men had killed off a six-pack of Bud Lite.

"We need to get back to our search," said Kit.

"I need to get back to mending some fence and earning my keep," said Buck.

"It was a pleasure to meet you, Buck."

"Likewise, Kit. I ain't too keen on outsiders coming into the canyon and roaming near the ranch, but I gotta tell you that you boys from Wyoming are welcome on the Sloan Ranch anytime."

Buck reached into his vest and took out a small spiral notepad. He produced a pen from the same vest and then wrote down a phone number. He tore off the page and handed it to Kit.

"This here is my phone number at the ranch. If you need access to the canyon from Highway 80, give me a call, and I'll let you through the gate."

Kit thanked Buck and placed the paper in his shirt pocket.

The three men shook hands and Buck got in the Jeep, fired it up, and drove off back the way he had come.

CHAPTER TWENTY

KIT AND THOR BEGAN THEIR search of Pine Canyon. Again they spent lots of time searching the many ravines and arroyos that ran down to the floor of the canyon. After a while, Kit began to go up one arroyo and then climb over and come down from the top of the next arroyo. This helped speed up the search, but neither he nor Thor found anything they felt was a clue as to the whereabouts of Leon Turner.

Kit's radio buzzed again. It was Swifty.

"What the hell happened down there?"

"It was just the local ranch manager checking up on what was going on. He's fine, and we're fine."

"Okay," said Swifty and he cut the transmission.

Kit and Thor used the radio call as an excuse to take a water break.

"How did you know all that stuff about this Slaughter guy?" asked Thor.

"I did a lot of research on this area before we left Wyoming," said Kit. "John Slaughter was a legend in this state and in the West. If Buck is kin to him, he's got a right to be proud about it."

The two men rose from their break and resumed their search of Pine Canyon. Two hours later, they had concluded their search of the canyon and walked back to the entrance to Skeleton Canyon. Once there, Kit radioed Swifty to let him know they had concluded their search and were headed back to camp.

It took almost an hour for the hot, dusty, and tired duo to finally climb back up to their camp. Swifty was about to greet them with a typical insult when he stopped short, his nose twitching.

"Wait. Is that beer I smell on your breath?"

"Beer?" responded Kit innocently.

"Yes, beer, you moron."

"Where the hell would we get beer in Pine Canyon?" injected Thor in an indignant tone.

Swifty looked puzzled. "You're right. It must be my imagination. I've been up here with two mules and two morons for so long I'm starting to imagine things."

Both Kit and Thor broke out laughing, and then they explained about the refreshment break they had with Buck Slaughter.

"I knew it!" said Swifty. "My nose has never failed me. Did you two even think about asking for an extra Bud Lite for old Swifty?"

"Never crossed our minds," said Kit with a straight face.

Swifty uttered an oath, spun on his heel, and went back to where the mules were tied off to check on their feed and water.

Thor whipped up a hot supper of beef stew from cans, but added fresh biscuits he made with a Dutch oven. The resulting meal was delicious and the biscuits came in handy to sop up the remainder of the stew, and the tin plates were wiped clean.

After they cleaned up the supper dishes, Swifty again produced three Cuban cigars and for the first time they made a small open fire near the mouth of the cave. The trio sat around the small fire which helped ward off the cold of the desert night. It was still amazing to them it could be so hot during the day and turn so cool when the sun when down.

"Isn't Big Dave supposed to get here sometime tomorrow?" asked Thor.

"Yes, and he is supposed to call me when he is about half an hour out of Douglas."

"If Buck would allow us to use the road in from Route 80, wouldn't that be a lot better than trying to haul everything overland from Douglas?"

"Thor, you're a genius. I can't believe I didn't think of that. I'll give Big Dave a call on the satellite phone right now. Then I'll give Buck a call, and I can walk down to the ranch and go with him to the gate to meet Big Dave. If Big Dave is bringing someone with him, I can tell him to go to Douglas first and pick up my truck and trailer and bring them to the gate as well."

"That would help enormously with supplies and setting up a good base camp," said Swifty.

"Where would be a good spot to set up the base camp?" asked Kit.

"How about Pine Canyon?" said Thor. "It's protected from traffic through Skeleton Canyon, and it's closest to the canyon entrance from Route 80."

Kit and Swifty looked at each other and nodded their agreement to Thor's suggestion.

"Pine Canyon it is," said Kit and he rose to walk to the cave and retrieve the satellite phone from his pack.

Kit got the satellite phone out of his pack and then walked to the highest point on the canyon rim, which was a short distance from the cave, to get the best possible reception on the phone.

Kit waited for the phone to make connections with satellites, and then give him a dial tone. When the phone was ready, he called Big Dave. Big Dave answered almost immediately. He was having supper in Tombstone, where he was staying for the night.

Kit explained the change in plans, and Big Dave told him he would pick up Kit's truck and trailer in Douglas and meet him at the Skeleton Canyon Road gate on Route 80 about ten o'clock in the morning. Big Dave had known where Kit kept a key to his truck hidden in a magnetic box inside the front bumper mounted winch. Big Dave told Kit he would call him on the satellite phone when they were leaving Douglas. Kit agreed and disconnected the call.

Kit looked at the phone and saw the battery power was at 50% capacity. Then he realized with the trucks in the canyon he could use them to recharge the batteries in the phone.

He punched in another number and waited for the call to go through.

"Hello?"

"Do I have the privilege of speaking to Ms. Shirley Anderson?"

"Well, if it isn't the wayward cowboy."

"How are you, Shirley?"

"I'm fine, even though this cowboy I met hasn't had the manners or time to give me a call since he left Boulder."

"Oops. I guess I plead guilty. I've really not been in a good place to give you a call until now. I'm sorry."

"Apology accepted. Where are you calling from? I have caller ID and all it showed was a call from Unknown?"

"I'm calling you from the south rim of Skeleton Canyon in Cochise County, Arizona. We set up a camp in a cave close to here and have been spending the last few days searching the canyon?"

"Have you found anything?"

"We've found nothing we can link to Leon Turner, but Big Dave is coming tomorrow with reinforcements to help with the search."

"My cowboy needs reinforcements?"

"This canyon has turned out to be a lot tougher place to search that I ever imagined. It's hot, dusty, and a truly nasty place."

"Based on what I know about that part of the country, I have no doubt you're telling me the truth. I need to thank you again for doing this and trying to help out my friend Leslie."

"I'm glad to try to help out."

"Well I really appreciate it. It says a lot about what kind of man you are."

"And what kind of man would that be?"

"The kind of man a girl can count on."

Kit felt himself blushing and he hesitated before he spoke again.

"You know it's kind of strange. During the day when we search it's a hot and crappy place, but at night when I'm sitting on the rim of the canyon looking up at the stars, it's also a truly beautiful place."

"I'd like to see it sometime."

"I wish you were here with me now, Shirley."

"I wish I was there, too."

"Well, I don't want to run the batteries on this satellite phone down so I need to say goodbye."

"Good night, cowboy. Be careful. I miss you."

"I miss you, too. I'll call you when we get out of here. Good night."

Kit disconnected the call and sat alone on the rim looking up at the stars. He did miss her.

CHAPTER TWENTY-ONE

THE NIGHT HAS PASSED WITHOUT any significant issue, other than another group of illegals passing through the canyon while Swifty was on watch.

The three men were up early and after a hot breakfast of eggs, bacon and biscuits, they cleaned up the dishes and fed and watered the mules.

Then they began repacking all of their gear and supplies. Thor and Swifty expertly loaded and fashioned all their packs on the two mules. They took their time leading the mules down the narrow trail on the canyon wall to the bottom. After arriving on the canyon floor without any serious incidents, they stopped to check the mules. Thor checked the packs and after he made a few adjustments, they began walking to the east, heading to the entrance to Pine Canyon.

About halfway to Pine Canyon all three men heard a loud thumping noise that sent sound vibrations through the canyon. They stopped in their tracks and stood transfixed as a Border Patrol Helicopter swooped down into the canyon and hovered just above them. Then the helicopter moved ahead of them and descended to the canyon floor after finding a good flat space with no rocks or trees that would endanger the copter's landing.

The helicopter's blades were still spinning when the passenger side door popped open and out came the now familiar face of Captain Vonalt. He was dressed in his all black uniform and black ball cap along with the mirrored sunglasses that must be standard issue with all of the Border Patrol agents.

He quickly walked up to the trio and shook all of their hands.

"Glad to see the three of you are still upright and breathing," he said with a wide grin.

"We've managed to get by," replied Kit.

"I can see that. Have you run into any more cartel thugs?"

"No, we haven't. We've seen groups of illegals going through the canyon at night, but no cartel dudes."

"Well I came out here to tell you we haven't found any clues as to who killed the six cartel men, and to warn you."

"Warn us about what?"

"Our intel boys have picked up some chatter in the past two days that suggest the cartel is really pissed about both the loss of their dope and the death of six of their men. They blame both on you boys."

"We didn't kill anyone!"

"You know that and I know that, but they don't. In addition, they don't know who you are, but they're trying to find out. Apparently their men are not eager to come after you in the dark after what happened last time. I don't know what they might try to do, but I felt I needed to warm you about what we heard."

"Thanks for the warning. Like I said before, we can take care of ourselves."

"I see you're moving your camp. Are you done with your search?"

"Nope. We're just moving the camp to a better place so we can finish checking out the entire canyon area."

"Have you found any clues as to what happened to the Turner guy?"

"We've found nothing that would suggest a link to Mr. Turner."

"But you're still going to keep on looking?"

"The job isn't done yet, Captain."

"I understand, Kit. Good luck and good hunting."

With that the captain gave them a salute by touching the brim of his hat, and he turned and walked back to the waiting Border Patrol helicopter. Seconds later the copter lifted off the canyon floor and within a couple of minutes the copter and its accompanying noise was gone from Skeleton Canyon.

Less than an hour later, they had reached the entrance to Pine Canyon. After a brief search of the canyon, they decided on a good location that was flat and had the shelter of a stand of juniper trees for at least some semblance of shade.

They unloaded the mules and then left them hobbled to search for what forage they could find on the canyon floor. It took less then forty-five minutes to unpack gear and supplies. Kit and Thor set up two sections of canvas they tied together and placed on poles as an elevated lean-to for additional shelter from the sun.

Kit then pulled out his satellite phone and made sure it was working properly. After he was satisfied, he placed it on top of their food pack and took a water break with Thor and Kit. While Thor and Kit had been setting up camp, Swifty had done a careful search of the canyon area around their campsite.

When Swifty returned from his search and joined the others for a water break, his shirt was soaked with sweat.

"Find anything worth all that sweat?" asked Thor.

"I didn't find a sign of anything other than the tracks of some small animals and birds."

"I take it that's a good sign," said Kit.

"You take it right," replied Swifty.

After drinking his fill of water, Kit paused to look around the canyon that was now their new home.

"This canyon reminds me a lot of one I was in north of Kemmerer."

"When was this?" asked Thor.

"Today, it seems like it was a long time ago," said Kit with a faint smile.

"So do we start searching or wait for that damn phone to ring?" asked Swifty.

"We wait for Big Dave to call."

Almost as if on cue, the phone startled them with a loud electronic chirp. Kit jumped up and retrieved the phone.

"Hello. Yep, it's me, Big Dave. You're leaving Douglas now? I'll be down at the gate where Route 80 meets Skeleton Canyon Road. See you then."

Kit disconnected the phone and placed it back on the food pack. Then he stopped himself and picked up the phone again. This time he pulled out a piece of paper from his shirt pocket and punched in a phone number. After a few seconds he made a connection.

"Hello, Buck? This is Kit Andrews from Skeleton Canyon. Yep, we're still alive and kicking. My guys are just leaving Douglas, so I'll be walking down to meet you to get the gate open. O.K. I can do that. I'll meet you at the corral and water tank. That's a great idea. Thanks."

"What did Buck have to say?" asked Thor.

"He's going to meet me just outside the entrance to the canyon where the ranch has a corral and a water tank. He said to have one of you come with me and to bring the mules, so we can water them at the tank."

"That's a great idea," said Swifty.

Kit and Swifty left shortly, leading the two mules down to the entrance to Skeleton Canyon. Thor was left to guard the camp.

As they made their way east the canyon became more open, but more choked with brush and rocks. Kit noted that much of the brush around was cat claw and acacia. All of the brush was thorny or sharp. Driving a vehicle through this part of the canyon would be hard on the paint job.

"No wonder Buck was driving an ancient Jeep," thought Kit.

They finally came out of the canyon and were looking down on the ranch corral and water tank. The water tank was a large metal stock tank that stored water and served as a water source for livestock.

Parked next to the corral was Buck in the old Jeep.

Buck got out of the Jeep and shook both their hands. He motioned to the water tank with his hand. "Take the mules over there and let them drink their fill. If you want to use the tank while you're camped in the canyon, help yourselves."

"What do we owe you for use of your water, Buck?" asked Kit.

"You already paid for the water by kicking those damn Mexicans out of the canyon. I feel like I owe you, not the other way around."

"Thanks Buck. It's truly appreciated," said Kit.

"No problem," said Buck. "Someday I may need your help."

"You call, and we'll be there," said Kit.

Buck just laughed.

Kit and Buck got in the Jeep and headed down Skeleton Canyon Road, leaving Swifty to deal with the mules.

The road was not paved, but it was in good condition and they soon were stopped by the locked gate. Both men exited the Jeep and Buck quickly opened the padlock, but left the gate closed.

Kit looked around and saw a house on the south side of Skeleton Canyon Road. The house fronted on Route 80, a two lane paved highway. To the north were three or four nondescript houses in various states of disrepair.

Buck saw where Kit was looking.

"That there is the thriving metropolis of Apache, Arizona."

"That's a town?" said Kit as he looked at the nearby roadside sign marked, Apache.

"That's what the sign the state boys put up says. And of course, it must be a town because them state boys are always right."

Both men burst into laughter.

Also to the right was a turn-out with a pine tree shaped monument of stone with a stone base around the bottom of the monument. There were brass plates on the monument.

"That there is a monument to the surrender of Geronimo to General Miles. It's here for the tourists. The real site is up on the canyon, just above where the corral and water tank are located.

I'll show you when we go back. It's marked by a pile of rocks."

"I'd appreciate that, Buck," said Kit.

Ten minutes later Kit's pickup truck and horse trailer, along with two big ¾ ton pickup trucks towing trailers pulled off Route 80 and up to the closed gate.

Big Dave stepped down from the driver's seat of the first truck, and a man with a familiar face exited from Kit's pickup truck. Kit recognized Thor's good friend Chance Jackson as the driver.

There was no mistaking Big Dave. He tended to dominate any gathering. He looked like the Viking stock he descended from. He stood six feet four inches tall and weighed about 250 pounds. He had broad shoulders tapering down to a narrow waist. He had curly light colored hair, streaked with grey and piercing bright blue eyes. When Kit had first seen Big Dave, he thought he was looking at John Wayne. Shaking hands with him was an experience, as he had huge hands and they tended to engulf a normal sized hand.

Kit introduced Big Dave and Chance Jackson to Buck. Chance was a former pro football player, who had a mobile welding and blacksmith service in Kemmerer. Kit had met Chance by accident when he happened on him outside Kemmerer. Chance had truck problems and Kit gave him a lift to Kemmerer. Chance was also an old friend of Thor.

By this time, the driver of the third truck had made his way up to the gate.

Big Dave grabbed the newcomer by the arm and pulled him forward in front of the group. "This here is Chapman McKusker. He's the best tracker in the Rocky Mountains. I convinced him to give us a hand in finding this lost greenhorn in Skeleton Canyon."

Chapman Mckusker was an imposing sight. He was about fifty years old with light gray hair and a well-trimmed beard to match. He was tall and had broad shoulders, and he gave off a sense that he was both strong and powerful. He wore faded jeans and denim shirt along with cowboy boots and a dusty grey cowboy hat that had seen a lot of exposure to the elements.

"Howdy," said Chapman as he shook hands with Buck and Kit.

Kit waited for him to say something else, but that was the extent of his conversation. "This is a man of few words," thought Kit.

Kit took a look at the trailers the pick-up trucks were towing. He recognized Big Dave's pick-up and the enclosed double-axle trailer he was towing. McKusker's pickup was a white late model Ford F-250 with a large diesel engine. The trailer was a large boxy horse trailer with storage space in the front. The trailer was vented near the roof, but the sides were solid. The trailer, like the truck, was painted a matching white.

The introductions finished, Buck opened the gate and the trucks passed through on Skeleton Canyon Road. Kit drove his pickup with Chance on the passenger side.

Buck closed the gate behind the little convoy and waved his cowboy hat in salute.

Kit led the way up the road to the entrance to the canyon, where he brought his truck to a halt. He exited the truck and went back to the other two drivers and explained the nature of the road ahead to make sure everyone drove slowly and kept a good distance between vehicles, so the drivers could see what was coming next in the rutted and rocky road.

His directions delivered, Kit climbed back into his pickup truck and began to carefully navigate the narrow and tricky road into Skeleton Canyon. The nearby brush scraped against the passing trucks and trailers, but caused no serious issues other than some scratched paint.

The convoy slowly made their way through the canyon until finally Kit signaled an upcoming right turn with his turn signal and his arm outside the driver's side window.

Led by Kit's pickup truck, the convey entered Pine Canyon and then parked side-by-side near the stand of juniper trees where Swifty and Thor had set up camp.

All of the men exited their vehicles and went through the process of greetings and the introduction of Chapman McKusker to Swifty and Thor.

Big Dave and Chance began to unload their gear and supplies from Big Dave's pick-up and trailer. McKusker did the same from his pick-up, and then he went to the rear of his horse trailer, opened the rear gate and lowered the ramp.

He stepped into the trailer and reappeared walking down the ramp leading two large brown and white llamas by halter ropes.

Kit, Thor, and Swifty stared in amazement. All of them knew what Llamas were, but none of them had actually ever seen one in the flesh.

"Llamas?" asked Kit.

"Yep," answered McKusker.

"He uses them for tracking," said Big Dave. "They are well suited to mountain trekking and can carry heavy loads with no problems. They do better on natural forage than mules or horses."

Chapman led the llamas into the makeshift corral Thor had built for the mules. The mules looked curiously at the llamas, but otherwise paid little attention to their new neighbors.

The men spent the next half hour unpacking and setting up their gear and turning the rough camp into a more organized operation. Once the camp was set up to everyone's satisfaction, Big Dave called a meeting.

He pulled down the tailgate on his pick-up truck and used it as a table. He took out a topographical map of the canyon and laid it out on the tailgate, anchoring down the four corners of the map with small rocks.

"Kit, explain to us where things have happened and how much of this place you boys have already searched," said Big Dave.

Kit went to the map and pointed out where they were currently located. He showed where they had made their camp by the cave on the rim of the south wall of the canyon. Then he pointed out the location of the narrow trail leading down to the canyon floor. Next he pointed to where the grove of Arizona sycamores stood and explained how they intercepted the illegals and dope smugglers. Then he touched on the spot where they had intercepted the second group of smugglers and pointed to the two sites where the cartel ambushers had been located. Lastly, he put his finger on the spot where the six cartel men had violently died.

Finally Kit used his finger to point out the areas of Skeleton Canyon they had searched and then the locations of Pony and Pine Canyons.

"The hardest part is all of the arroyos and ravines that feed into the canyon floor. All of them have to be searched and that takes a great deal of time. I have no idea how we search all of the nooks and crannies of the upper parts of the canyon walls. If anyone has any better ideas, I am all ears."

A few seconds passed, and no one said a word. The enormity of the task was very evident from looking at the map and then looking up at the canyon walls.

Finally Swifty spoke. "You'd have to be a damn bird or eagle to even be able to look into all the holes and gorges in this place."

"Maybe that's what we do," said McKusker.

"We become birds?" asked Thor.

"I think I have something better than trying to become a bird," replied Chapman.

"This I gotta hear," said Swifty.

"I brought a drone," said the tracker.

"A drone. What the hell is a drone?" asked Big Dave.

"That's what the military has been using in Iraq and Afghanistan," said Swifty.

"You've got a military drone?" asked Kit.

"Not exactly."

"Well, what exactly do you have?" asked Kit.

"I built my own drone. There are lots of them out there for sale, but most of them are only toys. This one is custom built and designed to fly patterns I program into the GPS system."

"Patterns?"

"Think of it like programming a flight plan into an aircraft and putting it on autopilot. It's the same principal."

"Have you used this drone before?" asked Chance.

"I've used it several times and each time I've made modifications to it. The drone I brought is a fourth generation drone."

"How exactly does this here drone thing work for us in this canyon?" asked Big Dave.

"I program the drone to fly slow patterns over areas of the canyon. During the day the drone has a camera that sends us a live video feed of what it sees below it. We watch the video on a large monitor on the ground. If we see something we want to look at again, I can take it off autopilot and manually change the course and control it like I was the pilot."

"How fast can it fly?" asked Swifty.

"Fast is not what we want for this job. We fly it slow and low to allow us to get good pictures from the video."

"How can you get streaming video from a camera when there are plenty of things in the canyon that could block the drone's transmission. Isn't this thing transmitting by line of sight?" asked Kit.

"You're correct. Transmission is by line of sight."

"Then how would it work?" asked Kit.

"We send up a tethered weather balloon with a transmitting and receiving device on it. The balloon is higher than the rim of the canyon and allows a sight line from the drone and then down to us on the canyon floor."

"Can you use this thing at night or only during the daylight?" asked Swifty.

"Good question, Swifty. The video camera is worthless at night because it can only show us what it sees, and it can't see any better in the dark than we can."

"So, we can't use it at night."

"Actually, we can use it at night. Only this time we take out the video camera, and we use a thermal imaging camera. We look for heat sources. We have to wait a little while so all the rocks in the canyon cool off and don't give us a false signal, but then we launch the drone and use the same autopilot method as we do with the video camera."

"I'll be damned," said Big Dave.

"There is one more thing we need to discuss," said Kit.

"What's that?" asked Big Dave.

"We need to be careful in this canyon. Lots of really bad things have happened here over the years, and it is a spooky place at night. In addition, we know we pissed off the cartel boys, and they could show up looking for revenge for what happened to those six dead dudes," said Kit.

"Anything else?" asked Big Dave.

"Actually there is one other thing," said Kit.

"Tell them what you found, Swifty."

Swifty looked up at Kit and smiled. "I searched the area around the Border Patrol's crime scene where the six bodies were found. I looked at one of the bodies, and there was no doubt he was killed with a blow to the head by an edged weapon. At first I thought it was an axe, but I've changed my mind. It was a tomahawk, not an axe."

"Why a tomahawk and not an axe?" asked Big Dave.

"In my search of the area, behind where the bodies lay, I found a patch of soft dirt. Most of the area is all rock. In this patch of soft dirt, I found a moccasin print."

Swifty got out his smart phone and pushed a few buttons and then showed the resulting photo image on the phone to the others.

"I'm no expert, but I'm almost sure that's a moccasin print."

McKusker took the smart phone and studied the photo. He looked up at the others. "That is definitely a moccasin print. You can see it is a little worn where the ball of the foot is. Indians walk with their toes down first, so they can avoid making any noise."

"Indians! Are we talking Redskins here?" asked Big Dave.

"Anyone can wear a moccasin, even a dumb white man, but who would wear moccasins in this rugged country? And only an Indian walks with his toes first,'" said the tracker.

"There is something else," said Swifty.

After taking his smart phone back from McKusker, Swifty adjusted it to show another photo.

"This is a shot I took of another moccasin print I found."

"Where did you find this print?" asked McKusker.

"I found this print about eighty yards west of our camp up on the south rim of the canyon. Thor said he felt like he was being watched on his part of the watch the previous night, so I went looking and found this print."

"Someone was watching you," said McKusker. He studied the print in the photo. "This is also a moccasin print, but it is a different moccasin, not the same one in the first photo. There are subtle differences, but the front is also slightly worn. It would appear to be another Indian."

The group was silent for a minute. Finally Big Dave broke the silence.

"Are you telling me that we got real live Indians on the loose in this here canyon? Indians that may have killed six cartel men with tomahawks. Indians that were scouting out Kit's camp for God knows what reason?" said Big Dave.

"I have no idea if we're dealing with real live Indians. It could be anyone, but why would they wear moccasins in this country, and why would they kill six men with tomahawks?" said McKusker.

No one had a logical answer, and no one spoke up.

Finally Thor spoke out. "You know, when Kit and I were talking to that Buck fella, he mentioned all the bad things that have happened in Skeleton Canyon and all the people who have been killed here. He said sometimes he felt like he could feel the presence of the ghosts of Skeleton Canyon. Maybe we're dealing with spooks."

All the rest of the men broke out in loud laughter. Even Thor joined in.

"Well, spooks or Indians, we still got a job to do and that's search this canyon for any signs of what happened to that Turner lad. I think we need to establish some rules while we're in this god forsaken place," said Big Dave.

"What rules you got in mind?" asked Chance.

"I think we keep a guard on duty every night and rotate the duty. I want everyone armed at all times. Keep a gun by your bedroll at night as well. Them radios we got don't always work in canyons. How many of them satellite phones do we have, Kit?"

"We have one," answered Kit.

"Well we brought two with us so that gives us three. One stays in the camp and one goes out with each search group. Nobody goes anywhere alone. There needs to be at least two of us in each search group."

"Does that mean I got to take Kit with me when I go in the bushes to take a crap?" asked Swifty with an evil grin.

"I think you can take a crap alone, but I'd make sure you took a weapon with you, and I'm not talking about that thing between your legs you're so keen on."

Everyone roared with laughter, and Swifty's face got bright red.

"If nobody has any other useful ideas, then I think we need to finish setting up camp and get some supper started. I suspect we lose sunlight pretty quick down here in the canyon with most of the west blocked off from us by the canyon wall."

The meeting over, the men scattered to take care of their gear and finish getting settled in their new camp. Thor and Chance elected themselves to get supper started.

Chance produced six rib-eye steaks from a cooler in Big Dave's truck, and he and Thor set out a supper of steak, beans, hash browns and biscuits. All of this was washed down with hot coffee.

While everyone else was helping clean up the supper dishes, Big Dave made a trip to his truck and returned with a small canvas pack. He sat down at the small campfire Kit had built and the rest of the men joined him.

"Did you bring some of them illegal Cuban cigars, Swifty?" asked Big Dave.

Swifty was mentally counting how many he had left in his stash and was worried about how long they would last with six of them instead of the planned three.

Big Dave looked at the concern on Swifty's face and laughed. "Don't worry, son. I brought my own supply, and he reached in the canvas pack and produced six Cuban cigars and passed them around. Very shortly all of them were puffing on their cigars after lighting them with burning twigs taken from the campfire.

"We'll draw numbers out of a hat to see who gets what shift on guard duty," said Big Dave.

He wrote numbers on pieces of paper and placed them in his cowboy hat. After everyone had drawn a number and figured out which shift they would handle, Big Dave reached into the pack and took out five pairs of G-3 high tech night vision goggles. He passed them around and explained how to use them.

"These look like the type we used in Delta," said Swifty. "I didn't think they were available to civilians. Where the heck did you get these, Big Dave?"

"Better you don't know, son. Kind of like these Cuban cigars. Don't matter where I got them, but it does matter that we do have them in a place like this."

Swifty smiled and shut his mouth.

After about an hour of conversation, the men retired to their sleeping bags, except for Kit, who had drawn the first watch.

Kit selected a site up on some rocks that were against the canyon wall and overlooked the camp and the entrance to Pine Canyon.

Thor came up to where Kit had established his watch location and sat beside him.

"Do you think we're really dealing with Indians in this canyon?" he asked Kit.

"I don't know if we are dealing with Indians, cartel thugs, fake Indians, spooks, or zombies, but somebody killed six of the cartel's men and they did it in a very personal and bloody fashion. For that reason I plan to stay alert on watch, sleep lightly, and keep my pistol in my sleeping bag."

"Sounds like good advice to me," said Thor. He said good night and returned back down to the camp below them.

CHAPTER TWENTY-TWO

THE NIGHT PASSED WITHOUT INCIDENT. No one on watch even saw any groups of illegals, let alone more drug smugglers.

"Maybe the word got out Skeleton Canyon isn't such a great place to travel through," said Thor at breakfast.

"Skeleton Canyon has never been a great place to travel through," said Swifty.

"It didn't seem to come up when I tried to get it on Trip Advisor," said Chance.

"What the hell is Trip Advisor?" asked Big Dave.

The other five men broke out laughing, much to Big Dave's puzzlement.

Big Dave knew he was being purposely ignored, so he changed the subject. "What's the plan gonna be for today?"

Chapman spoke up. "I'd like to take Swifty with me and take a look at the site of the two prints he found and also to look at the site where the six cartel guys were killed."

"Sounds like a solid idea. Take a satellite phone and keep in touch. Chance, you and Thor take the animals down to the entrance to the canyon and get them watered and then bring them back and feed them. You take a phone with you as well," said Big Dave.

"All of the livestock?" asked Thor.

"Yes, all of the livestock, including the llamas."

"How do I lead a llama? I ain't never been around one before."

"Lead him like a damn mule. He's just different lookin' and got a lot more hair. Now get goin'".

"What about me?" asked Kit.

"You and me are gonna hold the fort until the others get back. Make sure everyone goes out armed and keep your eyes peeled. Those cartel boys don't know where we are or how many of us there are, and I plan to keep it that way."

Within ten minutes both groups had departed, and Big Dave and Kit were left alone in the camp.

*   *   *

Deputy Vegas heard a signal his smart phone had just received a text. He pulled out the phone and after reading the text; he grabbed his hat and made his way out of the Cochise County Sheriff's office. As soon as he was out of sight, he hurried as he made his way to a coffee shop favored by yuppie gringos.

He bought a small black coffee and walked out to the patio in the front of the café and took a seat at one of the vacant café tables located there.

In five minutes, a short swarthy man came out of the coffee shop with a small coffee in his hand. He looked around and chose a seat at the café table next to the table where Deputy Vegas was sitting. The man was dressed in black jeans, a tan shirt, and worn cowboy boots. He wore reflective sunglasses and a St. Louis Cardinals baseball cap.

The man sat in a chair with his back to Deputy Vegas. The man sipped his coffee and said nothing to Vegas.

"Buenos dias," said Vegas softly so that only the man behind him could hear.

"Buenos dias, Deputy," replied the man.

"What can I do for you today?"

"You can provide me with some information, Deputy Vegas."

"What is it you wish to know?"

"A few nights ago some associates of mine were ambushed in Skeleton Canyon by some gringos."

"I have heard about that incident. According to the Border Patrol, six men were killed by blows to their heads with edged weapons."

"That's correct. We'd like to know who these gringos are, how many of them were involved, and if they're still in Skeleton Canyon."

"I think I can help you with that," said Vegas.

"What can you tell me, Deputy?"

"A few days ago three gringos from Wyoming came into the sheriff's office and asked about another gringo who went missing in Skeleton Canyon over a month ago. They said they were headed for the canyon to look for clues as to what happened to the missing gringo."

"Who are these three gringos?"

"They are three young cowboys from Wyoming. The one who seemed in charge was named Kit."

"Are these three undercover police or government agents?"

"No, I don't think so. They would have provided me with identification if they were. I think they are just three cowboys looking for a friend."

"So you wouldn't consider them dangerous?"

"I didn't say that. They are all big men and look pretty capable. One gringo might be dangerous."

"Why do you say that?"

"He had the look."

"What look?"

"He looked like ex-military, and he carried himself like he had been in some type of Special Forces unit."

"Did they have weapons?"

"I didn't see any weapons. They had a pick-up truck with a horse trailer behind it."

"They had horses?"

"No, they had two mules."

"Did you warn them about the canyon?"

"I certainly did, but they said they could take care of themselves, and I had the feeling they were not being foolish or cocky."

"So only three gringos are probably in the canyon?"

"I only saw three, and I checked at the desk of their motel and only three men had taken rooms for the night."

"Thank you, Deputy. You've been very helpful."

"Please, call on me anytime I may be of assistance."

"I'll remember that. I'm going to leave. Wait at least ten minutes and then go back to your office."

"As you wish."

The man picked up his coffee cup and walked down the street, pausing only to toss the cup in a nearby trash can.

After exactly ten minutes, Deputy Vegas rose from his chair and headed back to his office. His shirt was soaked with a cold sweat. He sat in his chair and waited for his heartbeat to return to a normal speed. He waited about fifteen minutes.

After Big Dave and Kit had finished policing up the camp, they walked up to the stand Kit had set up the night before. Here on top of a big rock they had a great view of the canyon and the entrance to the canyon, their backs against the canyon wall.

There was no shade as they sat with their backs to the west wall of the canyon. Both men pulled down on the front of their cowboy hats to shield their eyes from the blazing sun.

"It sure would be nice to have a few clouds show up today," said Big Dave.

Kit glanced up at the sky that was visible above the canyon walls. "It doesn't look very promising, Big Dave."

Big Dave nodded his head in agreement.

"I thought my dad might have come with you."

"He wanted to, but he had to take a flight to Washington, D.C."

"Washington?"

"Yep. Me and him went to Cheyenne to see the governor. The governor made some calls for us and got your dad a meeting in the capitol.'

"What kind of meeting?"

Big Dave didn't answer the question immediately. He pulled out a fresh cigar, clipped off the end, and lit it. Only after a couple of puffs on the cigar did he answer Kit.

"Well, you know your dad was working for the government when he got caught and thrown in that private prison."

"Yeah, he told me about that."

"Well, his contract called for certain kinds of compensation for his assignment. Apparently some bean-counter in Washington is refusing to pay on the contract, and your dad was pissed."

"Was the contract good even if he failed on the assignment?"

Big Dave took several more puffs on his cigar before he answered Kit.

"There were lots of provisions in the contract that paid your dad certain amounts even if he failed in his assignment, but this pencil pusher seems to think he can save the government money by screwing your dad."

"So that's why you went to Cheyenne to see the governor?"

Big Dave turned and spat on the rocks below him.

"The governor is an old friend of mine. I called him, and he agreed to meet with us and hear your dad out. When your dad got done telling him what happened, it pissed the governor off and he called both of Wyoming's senators and demanded they intervene."

"Did they agree to intervene?"

"Damn right they did. So your dad is flying to Washington to meet with one of the head honchos at the CIA."

"The CIA!"

"Who did you think your daddy was working for?"

"I guess I didn't really know who he was working for. I had no idea it was the CIA."

"Well, that's who he's goin' to see. Hopefully they do right by your dad. Pissing off your old man is a real bad idea."

"If they don't help him, what do you think he might do?" asked Kit.

Big Dave took a long pull on his cigar.

"If they was to turn him down and not help him, I wouldn't be buying any green bananas if I were them, if you get my drift."

"Really!"

"Your old man's a very dangerous man. He might be one of the most dangerous men on the planet. There ain't much I'm afraid of, but an angry grizzly bear and your old man are at the top of the list."

Kit shook his head in amazement. Big Dave reached down and picked up a canteen and handed it to Kit. Kit took a long drink and handed it back to Big Dave, who took a drink and screwed the top back on the canteen.

"Why do you say my dad is so dangerous?"

Big Dave paused before answering Kit's question.

"You sure you want to know why?"

"Yes, I am sure. He is my dad, even if I don't really know him very well."

Big Dave took a look around the canyon before he spoke again.

"I served under your dad in the army. He saved my life and the life of old Woody as well."

Woody was Harrison Woodley, an attorney in Kemmerer, Wyoming, who represented Big Dave, Kit's dad, and Kit.

"Your old man was the best soldier I ever saw. He could handle any weapon like an expert, and he could step into the woods or the jungle and just plain disappear."

"I once saw him take out a whole squad of the enemy with a pistol and when he ran out of ammo, he finished the rest of them off with his combat knife. Your dad is scary as hell when he's in a fight. I never seen anyone better, and I've seen more than a few tough hombres in my time."

Big Dave stopped talking and looked Kit in the eyes. "You heard enough?"

"I've heard enough. Thanks for telling me about all this."

"You need to understand your old man wanted to be here in the worst way, and he would be if he could."

"I understand."

"Good. Now if you'll excuse me, us old fellers need our rest."

With that Big Dave leaned back against the rock wall of the canyon, pulled his hat down over his eyes, and began to take a nap.

CHAPTER TWENTY-THREE

THE SILENCE OF THE DESERT land that made up the approach to the New Mexico end of Skeleton Canyon was broken by the buzzing sound of three dirt bikes.

The three riders were dressed in black and instead of helmets, they wore black baseball caps. From a distance they looked like they were agents of the U.S. Border Patrol. They were not.

The lead biker raised his right hand, and the three dirt bikes came to a halt next to a large clump of mesquite bushes. He motioned for them to shut down their bikes, and the other two complied. The lead rider was taller than the others and had broader shoulders. He was about five feet nine inches tall and had a lean, hard look to him. He was Mexican and he had a moustache and a short van dyke beard. He wore mirrored sunglasses as did his fellow riders.

The leader got off his bike and used the kickstand to park it. He reached into a saddlebag on the bike and pulled out a pair of binoculars. Using the binoculars, he scanned the area in front of the riders and on both sides of them.

"See anything, El Jefe?" asked one of the other riders.

The tone of the young man was polite, and he had addressed their leader properly with a logical question, but it still pissed off Francisco. He was not happy with this assignment. Being sent to scout out the location of some gringos in a place like Skeleton Canyon was bad enough. Having to take two green as grass young men who had no training whatsoever was a burden he did not appreciate.

Francisco was a former Mexican Marine, having served seven years and earning the rank of Staff Sargent before he deserted to take a much more lucrative positon with the cartel. He was twenty-seven years old and not happy with his two eighteen year old companions. He knew they needed experience, and this was the cartel's way of providing the experience on an assignment that did not sound too difficult when it was first explained to Francisco.

Experience had taught him the importance of obtaining accurate intelligence about the assignment, and he had done some research on his I-Pad back in Mexico. He knew that Skeleton Canyon was a bad place. He knew that twelve of the cartel's men had been sent to the canyon to ambush some gringos who had stolen a shipment of dope from the cartel. It was what he did not know that bothered him. He did not know who killed the six cartel men. He was told they were shot, but he had heard rumors that they had died much more gory deaths.

His assignment was to scout the canyon and determine where the gringos were and how many they numbered. He had been told there were three of them, but he was pretty sure that was old information. He knew from experience that anyone who relied on dated information did so at his peril. He was to sneak in the canyon, find the gringos, count them, and then slip back out of the canyon and report his findings using a satellite phone.

Doing this mission by himself would have been easier and safer than bringing along two worthless whelps.

After making two sweeps of the area with his binoculars, Francisco pulled them down and replaced them in the bike's saddlebags. He had seen nothing unusual and nothing that was moving.

He motioned to the two young men to join him. Heraldo and Jose immediately ran over to him. The two young men were like puppies in their eagerness to please the older and legendary Francisco. Francisco hated their fawning behavior. He had been told they could shoot the pistols they carried in holsters on their belts, but he wondered how they would do if someone was shooting back at them.

He explained to both of the young men they would ride to a spot about half a mile short of the canyon entrance, and then they would hide the bikes and approach the canyon on foot. He repeated the instructions to make sure they understood. Both of them nodded assertively that they did.

Ten minutes later he found a small arroyo big enough to conceal all three of the dirt bikes, and after parking them, he had the two cover the bikes with tumbleweeds.

They set out toward the south side of the canyon entrance, carrying only pistols and water. Francisco also brought his binoculars.

When they reached the entrance to the canyon, Francisco led them on a faint game trail that appeared to lead from the desert floor to the upper reaches of the south wall of the canyon.

The climb was not easy. The trail twisted and turned and sometimes seemed to disappear altogether. They stopped several times to rest and take water breaks. Francisco cautioned the others to ration how much water they drank. He knew there was no water in the canyon at this time of year, and certainly there would be none up on the rim of the canyon where they were heading.

* * *

When Swifty and Chapman reached the crime scene, the hot sun was baking the open area, as the north wall of the canyon provided no shade. Some of the yellow crime scene tape had torn loose in the wind and was flapping in the breeze like some medieval war banner.

Chapman pointed to the yellow tape. "Is this the crime scene?"

"It is."

"Where did you search?"

Swifty pointed out the area he had swept using a five yard wide path.

"Where did you find the moccasin print?"

Swifty led Chapman over the rocky ground until he came to an area about twenty yards northwest of the crime scene. He stopped on a flat rock and pointed down at the dirt in front of him.

"This is where I found the print."

Chapman stepped up to the flat rock and went down to his knees. His eyes flicked back and forth as he surveyed the small area of dirt that measured no more than and yard in diameter.

He then began to carefully move around the area of dirt and retraced where Swifty had searched. He had been slowly making his way in ever larger half circles to the north of the crime scene when he came to a stop. He knelt down and pulled a small wooden stick painted a bright hunter orange out of his vest and stuck it in the ground. Then he rose up and continued on his painstakingly slow search. Fifteen minutes later, he stopped again and once more he knelt down and pulled another bright orange stock from his vest pocket and placed it in the ground.

After almost an hour more of searching Chapman stopped at the face of the north wall of the canyon. He turned around to face where Swifty had remained standing.

"Do you notice anything, Swifty?"

Swifty looked at Chapman and then at the area between them. "I see you, and I see the two orange sticks you put in the ground."

"Draw a line between the two orange stakes, and what does that tell you?"

"The line points to the northwest."

"You're correct. I found another print. It would appear this is the direction that the attackers came from. Please come over here and use your camera to take a picture of this second print."

Swifty carefully made his way over the rocky ground to where the second orange stake was located. He looked down and sure enough there was a print he had missed on his earlier search.

He took out his phone and bent down to get a good photo of the print.

When he was finished, he stood up and discovered Chapman had appeared by his side. He had not felt Chapman's presence until he was next to him. If Swifty had any doubts about Chapman's credentials as a tracker, they were now banished from his mind.

"Can I see all the photos of the prints?" asked Chapman.

Swifty adjusted his smart phone and came up with the three photos of the moccasin prints.

"See how the first print and the third print are exactly the same," said Chapman.

Swifty could see they were identical.

"You're right. They're the same."

"I bet if we move to the northwest along the base of the south canyon wall we might find some more prints."

"I wouldn't bet against you at this point," said Swifty.

Chapman smiled at Swifty and motioned for him to follow his lead.

The two men walked slowly in a careful tandem as Chapman led the way. He found three other prints, and each time had Swifty use his smart phone to take photos.

After about forty-five minutes, Chapman came to a halt. He motioned Swifty forward with his right hand.

"Do you see that brown bush about ten yards to our right?"

Swifty nodded that he did see the bush.

"See anything wrong with it?"

Swifty looked carefully at the bush. "It doesn't belong there."

"How do you know that?" asked Chapman.

"It's a cat claw bush and everything along this canyon wall is mesquite."

"You're correct, Swifty. Let's see why it's been placed here."

Chapman carefully pulled on the large bush, both to avoid the sharp thorns on it and to remove it, so they could see what it might be hiding.

When the bush had been pulled clear and moved aside, both men could see the faint outline of a game trail that led up along the side of the canyon wall.

"I'll be damned," said Swifty.

"Well, that's not up to me, Swifty, but I'm guessing this is how the attackers got down to this part of the canyon to surprise the cartel men."

"So now what do we do?" asked Swifty.

"We could follow the trail up the canyon wall, but I'm thinking we might be better off if there were more of us, since we have no idea who, what, or how many might be up there."

"Sounds like a plan to me," said Swifty.

"Let's head back to the camp and let the others know what we have found."

Chapman reached into his shirt pocket and pulled out a piece of white chalk. He used the chalk to carefully mark four rocks on both sides of the trail. Then he carefully picked up the large cat claw bush and placed it back where they had found it.

"That should do it. There's no use letting anyone know this trail has been discovered."

Swifty led the way back to the crime scene. Once there, the two men set out for the entrance to Pine Canyon and their camp.

While they were walking back to camp, Swifty remembered something.

"When we first started out, we were also going to look at the print I found up by the cave where we first camped. Do you still want to do that?"

"Good catch. I'd forgotten about that print. We'll head up there after we stop at the camp to refill our canteens."

Fifteen minutes later, Swifty caught something out of the corner of his eye. They kept walking and Swifty waited to see if he could see it again. A minute later he did.

"Keep walking and act like everything is normal," said Swifty to Chapman.

"What is it?" whispered Chapman.

"I think we have company."

"What kind of company?"

"I'm not sure, but I saw a flash of light and after a minute I saw it again. It's up on the south rim of the canyon. I'm pretty sure it was the reflection of sunlight off glass. I'm guessing it's either from binoculars or the scope on a rifle."

"I don't like the sound of that."

"I think we're out of range of most rifles, and the downward trajectory would make this a tough shot."

"I'm not very excited about any kind of shot."

"We just keep walking and don't let on we know they're up there, and we should be fine. I think we're being scouted, not stalked."

Chapman replied by nodding his head in agreement, and the two men kept walking at the same pace and direction.

High up on the rim of the canyon, Francisco lay prone with his eyes glued to his binoculars. He could see the two gringos clearly. Both men walked like they had purpose, and both men were carrying pistols in holsters on their belts. They had the appearance of warriors to Francisco. He did not like the feeling he got watching them.

Francisco watched the duo until he saw them turn to the south and into what looked like the wall of the canyon. Francisco pulled a map out of his shirt pocket. He unfolded it and quickly determined they had turned into Pine Canyon, a side canyon to the south of Skeleton Canyon.

He stood up and motioned to his two companions lying on the rocks behind him. They rose and silently followed him as he moved west along the canyon rim.

About two hundred yards later, Francisco put up his right hand and the others halted. Francisco went to one knee and motioned the others to him.

"I'm tracking two of the gringos. They went into a side canyon, and we are changing positons so I have a better view of who might be coming and going out of that canyon. You two stay nearby and keep quiet."

Pablo, the younger of the two, stood up and pointed down the canyon. "They are just two stupid gringos. Let's go down there and shoot the assholes."

Francisco swiftly rose in one motion and in an instant he had Pablo's throat in his hands.

"You stupid fuck. You do only what I say. You keep your mouth shut. You only speak to me if I ask you a question. You open your mouth to me again, and I will kill you and leave your corpse for the coyotes. These men are not like the rabbits you have killed in Mexico. They are armed and experienced and likely they have killed men before. They would kill you as easily as they would step on an ant. You stay put and shut up."

With that Francisco roughly threw Pablo to the ground where he laid, trying to catch his breath and trying to relieve the pain in his throat.

Finished with the idiot child he had been forced to bring with him, Francisco moved to a prone position and began to scan the canyon are near where the two gringos had disappeared from view.

When Swifty and Chapman reached the camp in Pine Canyon, Swifty explained to Kit they were going check out what they thought might be someone spying on them, as they refilled their canteens. Swifty grabbed his M-4 rifle and tossed one of the captured AK-47s to Chapman.

"Know how to use this thing?"

"I certainly do. It's cheap, but very reliable."

"Let's go."

"Where are we going?"

"We're headed back to the trail that takes us up to the cave where we had our first camp up on the south rim."

"Lead the way, Swifty."

"You boys need any help?"

"Two of us should be plenty, Kit. Any more just makes too much noise."

"You boys take care up there," said Kit.

Swifty led the way to the entrance to Skeleton Canyon. From there he and Chapman hugged the base of the south wall of the canyon as they made their way west to the south rim trail.

Swifty set a brisk pace and soon they were at the base of the trail that led up to the cave camp. With Swifty in the lead, they were soon on the top of the south rim next to the cave.

"What now?" asked Chapman.

"We head south about fifty yards and then we make our way east, parallel to the canyon rim. My guess is that our company is watching the canyon floor, not their flank. With any luck we'll find them and provide a little surprise."

"I'm fine with surprises as long as they're not on me."

"I think you'll enjoy this one."

After about twenty minutes of brisk walking, Swifty held up his hand to halt their progress.

"I smell them," whispered Chapman.

"I'm not surprised," whispered Swifty. "I smelled them too. You stay here and I'll move up to get a closer look."

Chapman moved silently behind a large rock and went to one knee, holding his rifle at the ready position.

Swifty crawled forward, moving slowly and silently from one piece of cover to the next. Finally he was about twenty five yards from the canyon rim and he could clearly see one Mexican lying prone and watching the canyon floor with a pair of binoculars. About ten yards away were two young Mexicans sitting awkwardly on the rocky ground. All three of them had pistols in holsters.

Swifty reversed his direction and crawled silently back the way he had come. Finally he reached the rock that hid Chapman from sight.

"Here's the plan. There are three of them. One's prone and the other two are sitting. Their backs are to us. You take the right, and I'll take the left. When we get close I'll jump up and get the drop on them. You jump when I jump. Do you understand?"

"I'll follow your lead."

"Let's go."

The two men crawled forward slightly parallel to each other as they slowly made their way to their desired positons.

Swifty reached his spot and carefully looked to his right to make sure he could see Chapman. When Chapman came into view, Swifty gave him a hand signal and Chapman acknowledged it with a hand signal of his own.

Swifty gripped his rifle and took a deep breath. Suddenly he leaped to his feet and pointed his rifle at the three Mexicans.

"Hands in the air, mother-fuckers, or I'll blow your god-damned heads off!"

Francisco and the two young Mexicans were stunned by the sudden appearance of the very angry and armed gringo.

"You heard the man, assholes! Hands up!" yelled Chapman from the other side of the Mexicans position.

Francisco was no fool. He knew they had been caught with their pants down, and he recognized the two gringos he had seen in the canyon. He just couldn't believe they had gotten up to the rim of the canyon and behind him without him suspecting anything. How had they even seen him?

He spoke in Spanish to the two younger men, who both looked like they were pissing their pants in fear. Quickly they raised their hands to comply with the gringo's demand.

"Now get face down on the ground with your hands behind your head," yelled Swifty.

Francisco obeyed as did his younger companions who needed no translation to Spanish to understand what was being demanded of them.

While Chapman covered the three with his AK-47, Swifty moved among the Mexicans, quickly and efficiently relieving them of their pistols.

Swifty retreated five yards from the prone Mexicans and emptied the ammunition from the pistols and then tossed them on the ground next to him.

"Do any of you assholes speak English?" asked Swifty.

"Don't worry, Swifty, I speak pretty good Spanish," said Chapman.

"Ask the fuckers who they are, and what they're doing here spying on us."

Chapman translated the questions to Spanish and listened to the reply he got from Francisco.

Apparently Chapman did not like the answer he got to his question, and he slipped the selector level on his rifle to fire and pulled the trigger. A bullet hit the rocks about six inches from Francisco's head. Francisco quickly got the message and began talking rapidly in Spanish.

"That's much better," said Chapman.

"What did he say?"

"These boys are from the cartel. They were sent up here to scout us out. They're trying to find out how many of us there are and where we're located. Sounds like they were planning a little revenge raid."

"I was afraid it might be something like that," said Swifty.

THE GHOSTS OF SKELETON CANYON

"What do we do with them?"

Swifty thought for a minute before he replied. "My first instinct is to shoot them and leave their carcasses for the buzzards."

"That's probably not a good idea."

"It's probably not a good idea, but it's the one that appeals to me the most."

"So what's your second instinct?"

Listening to the exchange between the two gringos was making Francisco sick to his stomach. He did not want to die in this cursed canyon like so many had before him.

"Let's search them for any more weapons. Then let's march them down to the east end of the canyon."

"The east end?"

"That's the way they came up here by the look of their tracks. We take them back the same way. They came here looking for our camp and to find out how many of us there are. I want them leaving knowing nothing except they got surprised by two gringos."

"You mean take them as prisoners?"

"Only until we get them to the canyon floor. Then we call the Border Patrol and let them handle the Mexicans. They're illegal aliens in this country, and they're illegally armed."

"Good idea," said Chapman as he moved to pick up the three discarded pistols and place them in his backpack.

"Keep them covered while I search them," said Swifty. He thoroughly searched the three Mexicans, finding three knives and some spare ammo magazines.

When he was satisfied none of the three Mexicans had any other weapons, Swifty had them get to their feet.

"One more thing," said Swifty.

"What's that?"

"Tell them to take off their boots."

"Take off their boots?"

"It's a lot tougher to try to escape when you're barefoot."

Chapman laughed, and then he ordered the three to remove their boots.

Two hours later, a Border Patrol helicopter landed in the east entrance to Skeleton Canyon and took charge of the three Mexicans, along with their pistols and knives.

Before the helicopter departed, one of the agents came up to Swifty.

"Captain Vonalt says to say hello. He said to tell you officially to get out of the canyon and unofficially keep up the good work," said the agent with a wide grin on his face.

"Tell the Captain he's welcome," replied Swifty.

Then Swifty handed the surprised agent three pairs of boots.

"I wouldn't want to be accused of cruel and inhumane treatment," said Swifty with a grin.

The agent laughed as he took the boots and retreated to the waiting copter.

The two men moved quickly over the canyon floor and within less than an hour they were back at the entrance to Pine Canyon.

"Hello the camp," said Swifty in a loud voice.

"Howdy to the moron," came Kit's sarcastic reply.

"I didn't want to take no chance on getting shot by a nervous Nellie like you."

"I might just shoot you for the fun of it," replied Kit.

"What did you two boys find out there?" asked Big Dave, who was now wide awake.

"Chapman found more tracks and then he proved to me he is the best tracker in the Rocky Mountains when he followed them back to a hidden trail that leads up to the northern rim of the canyon."

"What did you find up there?"

"We didn't go up the trail. We figured it would be smarter to search it with a little more firepower than we had."

"Did you find any sign of someone spying on us from up on the south rim?" asked Kit.

"Thanks to Swifty, we found three Mexican cartel boys trying to find us."

"Did you catch them?"

"Like I said, Swifty is as good as advertised. He found them, and we snuck up on them. Swifty jumped up with his rifle and scared the shit out of those Mexicans. They were in shock at the sight of two pissed-off gringos with guns."

"What'd you do with them? They ain't here so I guess you did the right thing and shot the bastards," said Big Dave.

"Swifty and I took them down the east entrance to the canyon, which is where they came from. Then we called the Border Patrol, and they flew in a helicopter and picked up the Mexicans."

"You didn't shoot the assholes?" asked an incredulous Big Dave.

"No, we didn't shoot them. We did make them hike down the canyon wall with no boots on, though," said Swifty.

"That was smart," said Big Dave.

"It was easier than shooting them and then having to explain it all," said Swifty.

"Hello the camp."

All four men turned to see Thor and Chance enter the canyon leading the mules and llamas.

Both Chance and Thor wanted to know what had happened and Swifty and Chapman had to repeat their stories to bring them up to date.

"You didn't shoot the assholes?" exclaimed Thor.

"Ain't he a chip off the old block," said Swifty.

Everyone roared with laughter, with even Thor joining in.

CHAPTER TWENTY-FOUR

AFTER THE LAUGHTER HAD SUBSIDED, Thor and Chance took the mules and llamas to the make-shift corral.

"I had a good rest guarding the camp today, so I'll handle the supper chores. Kit, I'll need you to give me a hand," said Big Dave.

Soon Kit and Big Dave had a three-burner Coleman stove going and very shortly they were dishing out a supper of rib-eye steaks, fried potatoes, and canned green beans to a tired and hungry crew.

Everyone pitched in to clean up the supper dishes and soon the six men were setting around a small campfire, drinking hot coffee, and enjoying a fine Cuban cigar, courtesy of Big Dave. Big Dave then produced a bottle of Buffalo Trace Bourbon, and each man added a shot to his tin cup full of coffee.

"Chapman, why don't you tell us about this hidden trail that Swifty says you boys found by the crime scene," said Big Dave.

"Well, we found these moccasin prints in soft earth in several places, and we marked them with colored sticks so we could see if there was a pattern to the tracks."

"Correction. Chapman found the prints, and he figured out the trail using the painted sticks. I just followed along trying to figure out what the hell he was doing," said Swifty.

Chapman grinned at his tracking partner and continued with his story. "We followed the pattern, and then we found this cat claw bush in the middle of a thicket of mesquite and we knew it didn't belong there. When I lifted the cat clay bush out of the mesquite, we could see the game trail that led up the canyon wall. I'm guessing the trail leads to the rim of the canyon."

"So do you think the folks who killed them cartel boys used that trail to get down into the canyon and then back out again?" asked Big Dave.

"I would say that's probably what happened. Some of the prints were headed down to the crime scene and some were headed back to the trail."

"Any idea of who made them tracks?"

"Like I said before, the tracks are consistent with someone who walks with their heels down first, and the only men I've tracked who made tracks like that have been Indians."

"You're sure it's Indians?"

"I have no idea if it's Indians or not. What I'm telling you is that those tracks were made by somebody who walks like an Indian."

Big Dave stood up from the campfire circle. "I think we need to go up that trail tomorrow morning and have ourselves a look-see. I'll hold the camp with Chance and the rest of you take your rifles and plenty of water and two of the satellite phones. Give me a call every hour on the hour, so we keep in touch and make sure we know what's goin' on. Everybody savvy that?"

All five of the men voiced their understanding of Big Dave's instructions.

"Good. Then let's get some sleep. I'll take the first watch.

The five tired men headed for their sleeping bags, and Big Dave made himself comfortable on top of the big boulder that overlooked their camp. Then he set his rifle down and lit up a fresh Cuban cigar.

The night passed quietly with no alarms or interruptions in anyone's sleep. When Kit was on guard duty he ventured out of Pine Canyon and stepped into Skeleton Canyon. There he found a flat rock and sat down. He made himself comfortable and then he sat quietly. He listened carefully to the night sounds, and then he took in several deep breaths and tested the evening air with his nose. He could not hear or smell anything that seemed to be out of place. The only movement he could make out was a coyote loping across the canyon floor about a hundred yards away from his positon. Satisfied, he returned to his guard positon on the large boulder behind the camp.

Kit, Swifty, Chapman, and Chance awoke early the next morning to the smell of bacon frying and coffee perking. Big Dave and his son Thor had breakfast well in hand. The men soon sat down to a hot breakfast of scrambled eggs, bacon, sausage, fried potatoes, and lots of fresh coffee. Big Dave punched a hole in a can of condensed milk and passed it around to the coffee drinkers.

"Fresh from the tin cow's udder," he said with a grin.

The men finished their breakfast and were cleaning up the dishes when Chapman sat next to Big Dave.

"I been thinking about your plan from last night to get to the top of the rim and see what's up there."

"You got something better in mind?"

"Actually, I think I do. I think it's time to break out my drone and let it have a look at what's waiting for us on top of that rim."

"The drone can do that?"

"The drone has a video camera attached and it would allow us to see what's up there with no risk of getting our asses shot off."

"That sounds like a better plan to me. I'm kind of fond of my ass, old as it is."

"I'll need someone to help me get it ready."

"Pick whoever you want to help you. I doubt you'll have any reluctant volunteers."

Chapman chose Swifty. The two men went to the back of Chapman's trailer, and Chapman unlocked it and opened up the rear door. He motioned to Swifty, and the two of them took out a large square plastic container. Then they removed a five foot long cylinder with a valve on the top. Finally they took out a large plastic container that was about five feet by five feet and about eighteen inches high. Lastly they took out what looked to be an aluminum briefcase along with a smaller aluminum case with handles.

Chapman and Swifty took the large square plastic container and carried it to a spot about in the center of Pine Canyon. Then they carried the long cylinder with the valve to the same spot. Chapman produced a short handled mall from the truck along with a long metal rod with an eye at the end of it. He told Swifty to drive the rod into the hard canyon floor until it was only about eight inches above ground.

He left Swifty pounding the rod into the hard ground and returned with the small aluminum case. He opened the case and took out a black box about eight inches around. The box was covered with a hard rubber surface.

Chapman then opened the large plastic container and removed the contents. Soon he had what looked like a large piece of fabric attached to a very thin, but strong looking cable wound around some kind of wheeled device.

He took the black box and inserted fresh batteries he produced from inside the aluminum case and then he proceeded to test it. Satisfied with the resulting tests, he attached the black box to a connecting point just below where the fabric was attached to the cable.

"Are you done with the rod, Swifty?"

"I'm as done as I can be. It sticks up about eight inches from the ground like you asked."

Chapman then took the end of the cable, which was connected to the wheeled device, and attached it to the protruding eye of the rod.

He tested the connections of the cable to the rod and the cable to the fabric as well where the black box was connected. Satisfied, he turned to Swifty.

"Bring that tank of gas over here next to the fabric, Swifty."

Swifty lifted the tank and brought it over to where Chapman and the fabric were located.

Chapman produced a hose about six feet long and attached one end to the tank and the other end to a connection in the fabric.

"Are you ready, Swifty?"

"Ready for what?"

"This," said Chapman. He turned the valve on the tank and the fabric underwent a sudden change. At first it was just a pile of fabric lying on the ground. In a few seconds it had started to inflate, and within minutes it was becoming a very large balloon.

"What in the wide world of sports is that thing?" exclaimed Swifty.

"That, my friend, is a weather balloon. As soon as it's inflated, it will rise up and pull the wire cable with it until it reaches the end of its tether."

Swifty watched in amazement as the balloon inflated and began to rise in the air, unspooling the cable from the wheeled device attached to the rod Swifty had pounded into the desert floor.

"Jesus, how damn high does that thing go?"

"The cable length on this is four thousand feet. That box attached is a transmitter and receiver so we can control the drone anywhere in and around the canyon."

Fifteen minutes later the balloon was almost out of sight from the camp.

"Ready for the next step, Swifty?"

"After this I'm ready for anything."

They returned to where they had left the larger black plastic container and the aluminum briefcase.

Chapman opened the briefcase and after checking the batteries, he turned on what was a portable computer with a large eighteen inch screen. He let the computer warm up and then ran some diagnostic tests. After about five minutes, he was happy with what he saw, and he set the briefcase down on the ground.

With Swifty's help, they opened the latches on the larger black box and removed the top. Settled in the bottom of the box in a plastic foam bed was a large square drone. The drone was silver. It was about four feet by four feet with large helicopter like rotors at each corner.

Swifty helped Chapman carefully remove the drone and place it on the ground. Chapman checked the drone over and checked the batteries. Then he took a small black camera device from the aluminum box and attached it to the framework on the underside of the drone.

The two men then lifted the drone and carried it over by the aluminum brief case placing it carefully on the ground. Chapman picked up the briefcase, opened the computer, and turned it on. He began to enter data into the computer.

"What are you doing, now?" asked Swifty.

"I'm uploading a flight plan for the drone, so it will fly over the north rim of the canyon in the area where we think the trail we found might lead."

Swifty had no response that that.

By now the five other men had gathered around the motionless drone, waiting to see what would happen next.

Chapman had finished with all his data loading and testing. "Showtime, guys," he said.

Chapman was sitting on the ground with the computer in his lap. Suddenly the rotors on the drone began to turn and emit a loud buzzing noise. The drone rose into the air to a height of about ten feet and hovered there above the group of disbelieving men.

On a signal from Chapman, the drone rose another twenty feet and then began to move toward the canyon entrance, rising ever higher as it moved. Soon the drone was over the rim of Pine Canyon and continuing to rise higher. It turned to the north and suddenly accelerated and was quickly out of their view.

"Did we lose the damn thing?" asked Big Dave.

"No, we didn't lose it. I have it here and, as you can see on my screen, its sending back video of what is below it. The drone had reached the starting point of the flight plan Chapman had loaded, and it was slowly going back and forth over the rocky land that made up the north rim of Skeleton Canyon.

The men sat on the ground in a semi-circle behind Chapman, where they could see the images on the computer screen in his lap. The drone moved methodically back and forth along the rim of the canyon, sending detailed images of what was below it.

"What do we do if it actually finds something?" asked Kit.

"I can shut off the auto-pilot and control the drone with this joy stick on the computer," said Chapman.

The drone was moving laterally over the rim at a height of about twenty feet above the ground. After about five minutes, a picture of where the trail reached the rim of the canyon came into view.

"Look, there's where the trail reaches the rim," said Swifty.

'You're right, Swifty. Let's see where it goes."

Chapman brought the drone under his direct control and began to hover about eight feet above the trail. The video clearly showed several moccasin prints in the soft earth near the rim.

"Let's see where this leads us," said Chapman. He began to maneuver the drone slowly over the area in short turns, and in doing so, he managed to find other prints leading away from the rim to the northwest. He used the drone to follow the trail for about one hundred yards and then the ground got so rocky he was unable to find anymore prints. He maneuvered the drone in ever widening circles around the last print he had seen, trying to cut the trail, but was not having any success.

He brought the drone up to a height of twenty feet and had it hover.

"Maybe we need to let it get higher and see if we can see anything that looks like it might be a destination for the trail," suggested Kit.

"That sounds worth a try," said Chapman. He moved the drone higher and had it slowly turn in a three hundred and sixty degree circle. Nothing came into view that seemed to stick out.

"Take it up higher," said Kit.

Chapman elevated the drone to a height of two hundred feet above the rim of the canyon. Then he turned the drone slowly in a complete circle. They still could see nothing that looked distinctive.

Without any further suggestions, Chapman took the drone up to a height of five hundred feet and still nothing appeared on the video screen that seemed different.

"Well, that dang thing shows us there ain't no bloodthirsty savages waiting for us up at the top of the rim. Let's let Chapman work his stuff like we planned, and I'll stay with him. The rest of you get going and get up that trail and see what you can find on foot. Remember to check in on the satellite phones every hour on the hour. Remember to take plenty of water and don't forget them rifles," said Big Dave.

Within fifteen minutes all four of the men were equipped and headed out of the camp. Big Dave got himself a box from the camp and placed it near Chapman. He then sat on it and watched the video feed from the drone with an outdoorsman's curiosity.

"Can you put guns on that thing?" asked Big Dave.

Chapman laughed. "It would have to be a pretty tiny gun. You need a lot bigger drone to carry any kind of weapons system."

"You mean you can get a drone big enough to carry weapons?"

"You can, but you'd probably have a big problem with Homeland Security."

"What them boys don't know, can't hurt them," said Big Dave.

Chapman chuckled to himself and finished resetting the autopilot on the drone. The drone resumed its pre-programmed flight plan.

With Swifty in the lead the four armed men marched quickly across the canyon. Within half an hour, they came to the location of the cat claw bush and the hidden trail. Swifty carefully pulled the large bush out of the way and then led the men up the narrow game trail.

When he reached the top, Swifty moved to the side and unslung his rifle to take a defensive positon for the other three climbers.

All four of the men reached the rim of the canyon without incident and they began to follow the trail they had seen from the drone's video camera. Swifty was in the lead with the others following him in single file, each man keeping a distance of five yards between him and the man in front of him.

Twenty minutes later, they came to the last known location of a moccasin print. The ground was rocky, and they could see no sign of any more prints.

Swifty regrouped the men and using five yard intervals, he had them move forward from the left side of where the trail had ended. They moved slowly through the rocks and brush, each man carefully looking for any kind of sign that might indicate a trail.

Suddenly Chance threw his right hand up in the air and came to a stop. The other three men froze in their positions. Chance had been on the far left of the group. He went down to his knee and after a few seconds, he rose to his feet again. He signaled for the others to join him.

When the other three men reached Chance, he silently pointed to a large mesquite bush to his right. At first it just looked like any of the other numerous bushes they had already walked past. On closer observation, it was apparent that the dirt around the edges of the bush had been disturbed.

Motioning for the other men to cover him, Chance knelt down and reached around in the dirt. His fingers quickly found the edges of a piece of ¾ inch plywood painted brown. The bush, including roots clumped with dirt, came up with the plywood. As Chance raised the plywood, a sizeable foxhole became visible.

"Holy crap," said Thor. "That's a damn spider hole."

"Spider hole?" asked Chance.

"The Viet Cong had these hiding holes all over Vietnam. We were trained to look for spider holes when I got sent to the Gulf. We never found any, but I think they found Saddam Hussain hiding in a spider hole."

"Is there a tunnel attached to it?" asked Kit.

"Let's find out," said Swifty.

Swifty handed his rifle to Kit and lowered himself down into the hole. He had a small flashlight in one hand and his pistol in the other.

"See anything?" asked Chance.

"I'll be damned. There is a tunnel down here, but it's small. I'll have to crawl to get through it."

"Maybe that's not such a good idea. No telling what might be down there," said Chance.

"Only one way to find out," said Swifty and he disappeared into the blackness at the bottom of the spider hole.

The other three men stood around the top of the spider hole, waiting to hear something from Swifty.

They waited for fifteen minutes and heard nothing.

"This waiting sucks," said Thor.

"I hope Swifty doesn't get stuck down there. How the hell would we get him out?" said Kit.

"I'm pretty sure Swifty would use his knife and dig himself out, plus I'm sure we'll hear him yelling if he needs us," said Chance.

Another fifteen minutes went by, and with each passing minute Kid got more anxious for his friend.

"Are you boys looking for gold in that hole?"

All three men spun around to face the rim of the canyon from where they had just come. There, standing on a rock was Swifty, slightly the worse for wear and covered with dirt from head to toe.

They ran over to Swifty and yelled and pounded him on the back, raising clouds of dust.

"What do you mean, scaring the shit out of us, you dumb bastard," said Kit.

"I just lost five years of my life, and for me that's more than I can afford," said Thor.

"Stupid moron," said Chance.

Swifty just grinned at them.

"Look at this hole by this large rock. It's another spider hole. They laid on the edge of the rim of the canyon to watch what was going on, and then they used this tunnel to get back off the rim without the chance of being seen, even by someone on the opposite rim," said Swifty.

"Apparently they were a little smaller than you, Swifty," said Kit.

"Apparently, but probably not a lot smaller than me."

Kit took out his portable GPS and after activating it, he marked the two spider holes as waypoints on his system. Swifty nodded his approval.

"Let's head back to camp. I got the feeling we are looking for some folks who don't want to be found, and they are pretty good at staying not found," said Swifty.

The others agreed, and they made their way to the trail on the rim and headed back down the canyon wall.

Chapman had redirected the drone to do an over fly of where he had last seen Kit and the rest on the rim of the canyon. Within a few minutes the drone was sending back digital video images of the four men descending the game trail from the rim of the canyon.

"It looks like the boys are headed back to camp," said Chapman to Big Dave.

"I hope to hell they found something we can use. So far all we've seen with your drone thing is a lot of nothing."

"My sense is that we are dealing with folks who don't want to be seen, and so far they are succeeding," replied Chapman.

Big Dave just grunted his disapproval at the progress being made.

A little over an hour later the four men made their way back into the camp. They were hot, tired, thirsty, and in Swifty's case, filthy.

"What in tarnation happened to you, Swifty? You look like you been making love to a pig," said Big Dave.

That comment brought a big laugh from the other four men and a beet red face from Swifty.

"I found a damn tunnel up on the rim."

"Why the hell didn't you say so? I ain't no mind reader," retorted Big Dave.

"Tell me about this tunnel, Swifty," said Chapman.

"Chance found this odd clump of bushes and figured out it was setting on top of a hidden sheet of plywood. Under the plywood was a deep hole."

"You mean like a spider hole in "Nam?" said Big Dave.

"It was not only a spider hole, but it had a tunnel leading back toward the rim of the canyon. I got down in it, and it was darker than a black cat's butt on a moonless night. I crawled through it with a flashlight in one hand and my pistol in the other. The tunnel was small, but straight, and I came out in another spider hole that was right next to a large rock by the rim of the canyon."

"Was there any sign of recent activity in the tunnel, Swifty?" asked Chapman.

"It was pretty well packed down dirt, and so I guess the answer is yes. I managed to get a little dirty down there."

"We can see that, Swifty. You don't smell none too good either," said Big Dave.

Swifty lifted his arms to his nose and wrinkled his nose at the result. "Whew!" he said.

"You go over to the water storage and take yourself a cowboy shower. Don't spare the soap," said Big Dave.

Swifty looked down at himself and quickly made his way over to the water tanks. He had heard enough from Big Dave.

"Everybody get some water and let's have ourselves a pow-wow over here by this big rock," said Big Dave.

Ten minutes later, all six of the men were sitting on the ground in a semi-circle including a still damp, but newly clothed Swifty.

"Let's take us a look at the facts we currently have," said Big Dave.

"We know somebody who wears moccasins and walks like an Indian killed six cartel men with tomahawks," offered Thor.

"We know they came down from the north rim of Skeleton Canyon on an old game trail, and they went back the same way," said Chance.

"We know they developed a tunnel from the rim of the canyon to an area further in from the rim of the canyon, so they could move to and from the rim without any risk of being seen, even from the southern rim," added Kit.

"Why did they develop a tunnel to use a game trail when they could have just come down the canyon from the east end or from the west end?" asked Chapman.

"Why did they kill the Mexicans?" asked Big Dave.

"We know they scouted our original camp. Why did they leave us alone?" asked Kit.

"Did these unknown people have anything to do with the disappearance of Leon Turner?" asked Chapman.

"Those are all damn good questions, but I got another. We been usin' Chapman's drone and while it takes real good pictures, it ain't shown us hide nor hair of any of these mysterious Indians or whatever they are," said Big Dave.

"What if these people are not bringing in things from Mexico? What if they're getting stuff from the States and taking to a place in Mexico?" said Kit.

"You mean like they slip into the U.S from Mexico and enter from New Mexico into the canyon and then take a trail up to the north rim instead of going through the canyon into Arizona?" said Chance.

"Maybe we got ourselves some sort of outlaws who have a hideout in Mexico, and they slip into the U.S. and get supplies and then slip back into the Sierra Madre Mountains in Mexico," said Big Dave.

"That would explain the trail and the tunnel. I couldn't figure out why you would dig a tunnel when you could just walk through the canyon at night. If they went through the canyon, they could be seen by ranchers or the Border Patrol," responded Kit.

"I think the answer to Big Dave's question about why the drone hasn't found anything might have to do with the method these unknown folks are using," said Chapman.

"What method is that?" said Big Dave.

"Like I said before, we are dealing with folks who don't want to be seen, and they are damn good at it. I think they killed the six Mexicans because there was some sort of conflict between the two groups. I don't know what it might be, but we know the cartel doesn't like competition of any kind. Maybe this group is seen by the cartel as competition. We know the cartel is pissed offs by us being here and by what we have done to some of their men. We know the cartel is trying to locate us and estimate our strength. I'm pretty sure we haven't heard the last from the cartel, and we need to be careful."

"Are you saying that this other group depends on getting supplies from Arizona into some place in the Sierra Madres where they have a hideout?" asked Kit.

"I'm beginning to suspect that we are actually dealing with Indians, and if so, we are probably dealing with a mysterious group known as the Bronco Apaches."

"Who the hell are the Bronco Apaches?" asked Big Dave.

"I've heard stories of renegade groups of Apaches that are called Bronco Apaches living on the border between Arizona, New Mexico, and Mexico," said Chapman.

"That sounds like hogwash. Geronimo and his Apache band surrendered back in 1886. The rest of his trip got shipped off to Florida, and they never returned to Arizona," said Kit.

"History says otherwise," said Chapman.

"What history?" asked Kit.

"The last fight between the U.S Cavalry and the Apaches took place in the Bear Valley in Arizona in 1918. The last known Apache raid into the United States occurred in the fall of 1924. The last known Apache renegade was killed by the Mexicans in 1935. Who is to say that ended the presence of the renegade Apache in Arizona? One thing is for sure. We are dealing with some kind of group of Indians, and this has been Apache country for hundreds of years," said Chapman.

"So how does that help us?" asked Big Dave.

"It doesn't help us, but it tells us we need to take another tack to get our answers."

"Tack? What the hell is a tack?" asked Big Dave.

"Tack means direction. We need to take another direction."

"I still don't know what the hell you're talking about, Chapman."

"I think we need to recharge the drone and change the video camera to thermal imaging and send it up after it gets dark tonight."

"What exactly does thermal imaging do?" asked Chance.

"It lets us see in the dark," said Kit.

"Not exactly see in the dark, Kit. It shows us where sources of heat are located. We wait until the rocks have cooled off from the day's heat, and then if there is any living thing on the ground, the drone will see it," said Chapman.

"Sounds like a plan to me," said Kit.

"If it means we're doing somethin' instead of just twiddling our thumbs, then I'm for it," said Big Dave.

Thor volunteered to get supper going, and Chance agreed to help him. Kit and Swifty went to get the mules and llamas to take them down to the ranch's stock tank for water. Big Dave stayed to watch Chapman get the cameras on the drone changed out.

Deputy Vegas had just returned from his morning coffee break and was about to pull the chair out from his desk when he saw a plain manila envelope lying in the middle of his desk top. He looked around him to see if anyone was watching. Seeing no one around him, he sat at his desk and picked up the envelope. There were no markings or writing on the envelope. He ripped open the end of the envelope and found a single sheet of paper. On the paper was printed, "Coffee, 10 A.M."

Vegas looked around the room and still saw no one looking at him. He quickly folded up the paper and slipped it into his shirt pocket. Then he took the empty envelope, folded it up and placed it in his front pants pocket. Looking up at the clock on the wall, he saw he had ten minutes. He slapped his hat on his head and swiftly made his way out of the sheriff's offices. He made himself keep to a walk, but it was a swift walk. He had no intention of being late.

He arrived at the coffee shop with two minutes to spare. He ordered a small coffee and sat outside at the same small café table as before. He had no sooner gotten seated when another man sat at the table next to Vegas. The man sat with his back to the deputy.

"Buenos Dias, Deputy Vegas," the man said in a very low voice that could only be heard by the deputy.

"Buenos Dias," replied Vegas.

"We have something we need you to do, deputy."

"What is it you wish of me?"

"Tonight there may be a call for law enforcement in Skeleton Canyon. You are to make sure that no officers from the sheriff's department respond to the call. Do you understand?"

"I understand, but I am not scheduled to work tonight."

"You will make sure there is no response. Do you understand?"

"I will be in the office tonight, and I will make sure there is no law enforcement response."

"Excellent. Now please leave."

Deputy Vegas quickly rose to his feet, almost spilling his coffee in the process. As he made his way back to the sheriff's office, his stomach was doing flip-flops. He was going to have to explain to his wife why he could not take her out to dinner tonight as he had promised. He was not looking forward to calling her with the bad news. He also knew he could not afford not to be in the office, and under no circumstances could he allow anyone from the sheriff's department to be anywhere near Skeleton Canyon on this night.

CHAPTER TWENTY-FIVE

K IT AND SWIFTY WERE WALKING back to the camp, leading the mules and the llamas they had just watered at the ranch's stock tank.

"You think there's any truth to those stories Chapman was telling us about these Bronco Apaches?" asked Swifty.

"I have no idea. I never heard of any Bronco Apaches before, but this is a very strange place. I kind of get the feeling there could be almost anything in these mountains and particularly in this canyon. This is pretty rugged country. If a man wanted to hold up here, he would be mighty tough to find."

"I agree he would be tough to find, but how would he survive in here? Except for a short time each year, there's no water and while there is some wild game, we've been here for days and we haven't seen much. What would he do for food?"

"Maybe that explains why we found a trail that seems to be more for access to the canyon and to the east than to the west into Arizona. Maybe it's a supply trail like was suggested."

Swifty stopped paused to look in all directions around their position. All he could see was rocks, dirt, and sparse vegetation.

"I don't see how anyone could survive out here for a long period of time. It's a very unforgiving place."

"I've read where Geronimo's band, which was made up of renegades from the Chiricahua tribe, held out in the Sierra Madres for years. They lived in dome shaped homes made of brush," said Kit.

"What the hell did they eat?"

"Their primary source of food was deer. They also ate rabbits, possums, squirrels, and horses and mules when they could find them."

"That don't sound very appetizing to me. How the hell do you know all this stuff?"

"I read books, unlike some people I know."

"I read books," protested Swifty.

"You only read books with lots of pictures and usually pictures of young women in various stages of undress."

"What's wrong with that?"

Kit ignored Swifty and went on with his explanation of the Apache.

"That wasn't all they ate. They baked agave crowns, pounded them into pulp and made cakes. They took the fruit off saguaro, prickly pear, and cholla. They also ate mesquite beans and oak acorns, juniper berries, and pinyon nuts."

"I'm never going to an Apache restaurant."

"My point is the Apache lived in these mountains for hundreds of years. They lived in a place where the white man can barely survive. During the Apache wars, a cavalry officer said the Apache carried almost nothing but arms and ammunition. They lived on cactus and they could go more than 48 hours in the desert without water. They knew every water hole and every foot of ground in these mountains. They had incredible endurance. They could travel for weeks on foot at a rate of seventy miles a day. They were an amazing people. Their culture is something passed down from generation to generation. It's more likely that there could still be some Bronco Apaches in these parts.

Both men stopped briefly to watch a dust colored lizard skitter across the trail in front of them.

"For all that talk, how come we haven't seen any of these so-called Bronco Apaches after being in Skeleton Canyon for several days and nights?" asked Swifty.

"Just like Chapman said. You can't see people who are good at not being found. If they wanted us to see them, we'd be able to see them. In the old West, people in Arizona had no interest in seeing Apaches because by then it was too late. Now maybe the reverse is true."

"So if we do finally find these Bronco Apaches, do we shake hands or do we shoot them?"

"I think it all depends on what happens when we do find them," said Kit.

The two walked the rest of the way to camp in silence, which was unusual for both of them.

They returned to a quiet camp. Everyone was busy with their personal gear, including cleaning and loading their weapons.

After they placed the mules and llamas in the corral, Kit and Swifty joined their labors.

Supper was somewhat somber, with each man seemingly alone with his own thoughts as they ate.

Big Dave broke the silence as he stood up.

"Chapman is going to launch the drone about two hours after the sun goes down and the rocks in the canyon have cooled off. This time the drone is equipped with a special camera that can find images created by heat. What we're looking for is body heat. I think we need to talk about what we do if the drone actually finds something. Anybody got any ideas?"

Swifty looked around at the group and then stood up. "If the drone finds one person or a group, it doesn't do us much good unless we can contact them and find out who they are. I think we need to be ready to haul ass if we find anything."

"I agree with Swifty," said Kit. "We should have a response team ready to go."

Chapman looked around at the others and then spoke.

"I suggest we have a four man team, armed with rifles and equipped with the night vision goggles that Big Dave brought with him. They should also take two of the satellite phones. I suggest I go up on the south rim of the canyon with one of you. I can take the drone control with me. That way if we need to manipulate the drone, we can do it faster. I would take the night vision binoculars that Swifty has and the one who goes with me also takes a pair of the night vision goggles."

"That sounds like a good plan, Chapman," said Swifty. "I suggest you take Kit with you."

"Why me?" asked a surprised Kit.

"Because we just might need some long range help," replied Swifty. With that he strode over to the back of his truck and produced Kit's AR-10 rifle.

"I stuck this in the truck thinking we just might need something to reach out and touch someone."

Kit grinned in understanding. "I'll go with Chapman and provide oversight protection if you boys get called out."

"Kit and I will have the other satellite phone with us. If the drone spots something, we'll call you and give you the location and the coordinates so you can use your GPS units if you need to."

"So I gather that this ain't no outing for squirrel rifles," said Big Dave.

"I think we need the maximum firepower we can muster for this op," said Swifty. "I'll have my M-4 and we have two AR-15's and several AK-47s, although we don't have a lot of ammo for the AKs."

"I ain't shot much except for my 30-06 for years, and that rifle seems a mite under-gunned for this trip."

Big Dave walked over to his pick-up truck and pulled a long aluminum case out from behind the seats. He set the case on the bed of the truck and unlatched it. After opening the case, he removed a rather large and nasty looking weapon.

"What the hell is that?" asked Chance.

"This, my young friend, is a gift from my old pal, Mr. Browning."

Chance looked confused.

"What you see there, Chance, is a Browning Automatic Rifle or as it's better known, a BAR," said Swifty.

"A BAR?"

"It's basically a portable machine gun from World War I, World War II, and Korea. It chambers a 30-06 round and has 20 round magazines."

"This gun killed a lot of Chinese in Korea," said Big Dave.

"Do you have magazines for it?" asked Swifty.

Big Dave produced a chest pouch that held about twelve magazines, all filled with cartridges.

"That looks adequate to me, Big Dave. I'm just glad you're carrying that thing. If I remember correctly, it weighs about seventeen pounds," said Swifty.

"It weighs eighteen pounds when it's empty, more when it has a twenty round magazine in it," replied Big Dave. "If we get in any trouble, you'll be glad we got it."

"Of that I have no doubt," said Swifty.

CHAPTER TWENTY-SIX

ONE HOUR BEFORE DUSK FOUND Chapman and Swifty leaving camp with Chapman leading a well-loaded llama.

Big Dave and the others made themselves comfortable around the camp. All of them either wore tactical vests or carried small backpacks. They carried pistols in holsters on their belts and had night vision goggles on their heads, ready to be pulled down over their eyes. At Swifty's suggestion, all six of the men wore the darkest clothing they had. Swifty went around to each of them, checking their gear, and reminding them to check the batteries on flashlights, GPS units, satellite phones, and the red dot scopes on their rifles. Big Dave had already checked the batteries on the night vision goggles.

Kit's mouth felt dry as he led the way for Chapman and the llama. He had no idea if the plan for this night would be productive, but his gut told him it was unlikely to be quiet like the previous nights. His eyes and ears detected nothing out of the ordinary, but he noted the sky was partly overcast. He knew the coming night was likely to be quite dark.

Kit turned back to check on how Chapman and the llama were doing. They were right behind him.

"Did you check all the batteries on the drone and the portable computer?" he asked Chapman.

"I checked all that long before we left. We're in A-1 condition."

When they reached the trail at the canyon floor, Kit stopped and did a visual check of the rim above them. Satisfied that he neither saw, heard, nor smelled anything out of place, he started up the trail with Chapman and the llama right behind him.

When they reached the rim, they paused to rest and took a water break. Chapman took the opportunity to check the load on the llama, making sure nothing had shifted during the climb to the rim.

Their water break finished, they set out following the rim to the east until they reached the cave and the original camp. They stopped there and Chapman took out the night vision binoculars and scanned the rim to their east and the canyon floor below them. Even though it was still daylight, the binoculars worked in the light as well as the dark, and he was satisfied they were alone.

It took almost an hour before they reached the east end of the canyon rim. It was dusk, and Chapman wasted no time unloading the llama and getting both the drone and the computer up and running. When he was satisfied that all systems were go, he moved to the edge of the rim and sat down on a bare patch of soft soil.

Meanwhile, Kit had taken up a position near the corner of the rim where the canyon wall to the east ended. He sat on a flat rock and scanned the opposite rim and then the east entrance to the canyon with the binoculars. Lying next to him was his loaded AR-10 with the bi-pod extended.

Chapman slid next to the rock Kit was occupying. He held out a thermos.

"How about some hot coffee? It's gonna be another hour and a half before we can lift off the drone."

"I'll take a rain check," said Kit. "How about you take my place on watch, so I can take care of some personal business first?"

'Happy to oblige you, Kit."

The men changed places, and the thermos remained unopened and lying on the ground next to Chapman.

Kit walked back to where the llama was tied off to a vertical rock. He pulled the satellite phone out of his tactical vest and powered it on. After the phone had acquired the necessary satellite signal, a green light came on. Kit looked at his watch and then punched in a now familiar cell phone number.

"Hello."

"Is this the nurse on emergency call?"

"Well, if it isn't the long lost cowboy."

"Sorry for not calling sooner. Things have been a little crazy around here."

"Something tells me things are always a little crazy around you, Cowboy."

"Not all of the time."

"Too much of the time. Where are you?"

"I'm up on the rim of Skeleton Canyon on watch."

"On watch for what?"

"We're not sure. It could be Mexicans, it could be Indians, or it could be plain old ghosts."

"What's going on out there?"

"We think we may be dealing with a small group of renegade Indians called Bronco Apaches. We know we are also dealing with members of the Mexican cartel. The ghosts could be anybody."

"Very funny. Are you telling me there are still wild Apaches in that canyon?"

"We don't know, but we think it might be a possibility. We've found signs, but no proof."

"Don't tell me those Indians are the ones who killed the Mexicans in the canyon?"

"We think they might be the ones, but we can't tell for sure. The Mexicans are the only ones we're sure about."

"So you haven't found any clues as to what happened to Leon?"

"No, we haven't, but we think either the mysterious Indians or the Mexicans might know."

"How are you going to find out from them?"

"I honestly have no idea, but we are trying to make contact. If we can, we might get to stage two and ask some questions."

"Please be careful. I get the feeling what you're doing tonight might be dangerous."

"It's not dangerous. I'm just up here on the rim looking out at the scenery, while I drink some coffee. It's just like a walk in the park."

"I haven't known you very long, Kit, but I can already tell when you aren't telling me the truth. Please be careful and let me know what's happening."

"Hey, you're the one working in a hospital with all those germs and diseases. You're the one who needs to be careful. I'm just a lowly cowboy out here in the fresh air, trying to figure out what's going on around him."

"Nice try, Cowboy. I miss you."

"I miss you too, Shirley. I'll call you later."

"Good night, Kit."

"Good night, Shirley."

Kit disconnected the phone and placed it back in his vest. Then he returned to his spot on the rock and took the binoculars back from Chapman. Chapman handed him a hot cup of coffee, which he gratefully accepted. Kit knew the caffeine would come in handy during the long night ahead.

Two hours had passed since the sun went down to the west of the canyon, and Chapman had just launched the drone into the night sky.

"Does the drone have any lights on it?" asked Kit.

"There're no lights on the drone."

"So, we have no way to see where it is?"

"That's the idea, Kit. If we can't see it, then no one else can either. Besides, I'm watching the monitor and looking at what the drone camera is seeing."

"Duh, I finally get it," said Kit. "Can they hear the drone when it's over them?"

"They can't hear it, unless it's less than one hundred feet over their heads, and then it's just a low buzzing noise."

With a cloudy sky overhead and little to no moon or star light, the night was extremely dark. After the drone launched, neither Chapman nor Kit could either see it or hear it.

The satellite phone buzzed in Kit's vest pocket. He flipped it on and answered it.

"Kit here."

"Is anything happening up there?" asked Swifty.

"Not a thing is happening up here. We launched the drone about ten minutes ago and everything is quiet."

"We're getting bored down here."

"Do something useful, Swifty. Read a book, preferably one with very few pictures in it."

"Bite me, Kit."

Kit clicked off the phone and chuckled to himself.

"The boys getting bored down there?" asked Chapman.

"Swifty certainly is," said Kit.

"Better to be bored than being shot at."

"Amen to that, Chapman."

Kit abandoned his use of the night vision binoculars and sat next to Chapman where he had a good view of the drone monitor. The heat imaging camera gave a pretty good picture of the land it was going over.

"What are we looking at now?" asked Kit.

"We're looking at the east entrance to the canyon."

"Can we move it over to take a look at the north rim of the canyon?"

"Why not. I'll move it over there so we can have a look-see."

Chapman used a small joy-stick that was part of the computer controlling the drone. He disengaged the auto-pilot and directed the drone to the north rim of the canyon.

Jose Escobar put his hand up and brought the line of his men to a halt. He lifted his night vision binoculars to his eyes and he scanned the horizon to the west. He moved the binoculars back and forth in a scanning motion, as he looked carefully at all the approaches to the east entrance of Skeleton Canyon.

Jose did not like this assignment, but he had been ordered to carry it out and he would do so. To do otherwise would invite a slow and brutal death. As he studied the area before him, he began to formulate a plan.

He could not be sure anyone would be coming out of the east end of the canyon on this night, but that's what his bosses expected. He decided he would leave ten men in an arroyo located about five hundred yards from the beginning of the south rim of the entrance to the canyon to make sure no one escaped his ambush by fleeing into Mexico.

He would set up the remaining forty men in an L-shaped ambush running first parallel to the wall of the north rim from the canyon entrance to the east and then turning ninety degrees to the south. It was a classic infantry ambush, as he had been taught during his younger days in the Mexican Army.

Jose was not fond of night ambushes, but he knew they could be very effective and the element of surprise was multiplied by the darkness in creating confusion for the enemy. He also knew that night clashes could work both ways and be just as confusing for his men.

He wished his men were equipped with night vision equipment, but his binoculars were all he had. Another promise made and not kept by his bosses.

He took one last look at the entrance to the canyon and motioned for his two junior officers to join him.

"Diaz, you take nine men and take up a flanking position at the northeast facing arroyo we just passed. You know the one?"

"Si, Jefe."

"Diego, you and I will take the rest of the men and set up an L-shaped ambush extending east from the north wall of the canyon and then turning to the south. Do you understand?"

"Si, Jefe."

"Excellent. Tell your men to keep quiet. No smoking and no talking. You are to wait for my command to fire. Heraldo, I will call you on the radio if I see someone coming into the ambush. Your job is to make sure no one escapes the ambush. Do you understand, Heraldo?"

"Si, Jefe.

With that Diaz motioned to nine of the waiting men, and they moved quietly to the south. Diego led the remaining men in a silent line heading to the east end of the north canyon wall.

Jose took a deep breath. He did not know if they would be facing Indians or gringos or see nothing at all. He wanted to be successful, but right now he would settle for the latter choice of an uneventful night.

CHAPTER TWENTY-SEVEN

A S THE DRONE BEGAN TO slowly fly over the north rim of the canyon, Kit and Chapman watched carefully as the land slipped slowly by on the screen of the monitor.

"Wait! I saw something next to the rock we just passed over," said Kit.

Chapman turned the drone and slowed its speed. A heat shape appeared on the monitor, just where Kit had seen it.

"That there, my boy, is a coyote," said Chapman.

"Well, at least it's something," grumbled Kit.

"Good eye, even if it was just a coyote," said Chapman as he returned the drone to the original course of the preprogramed flight plan.

The drone continued doing a slow zig-zag pattern over the north rim of the canyon. In the next half hour Chapman and Kit saw two deer and what appeared to be a bobcat, but no Indians.

"I'm going to reset the drone to patrol outside the east entrance to the canyon," said Chapman.

"That's fine with me. We aren't having much luck up on the rim," replied Kit.

Both men watched as the drone responded to the change in flight plans and headed toward the end of the rim to the east and then continued out into the desert beyond.

The satellite phone in Kit's vest buzzed.

"Kit here."

"Is anything happening out there?"

"I'll call you just as soon as we see something, Swifty, and not before," said an exasperated Kit.

"Well, don't take forever. I'm running out of bullshit stories to tell these boys."

"Why do I find that hard to believe? Kit out."

Kit replaced the phone in his vest and reached for the cup of coffee he had left setting on the ground.

"Kit! Look at this!"

Kit slid next to Chapman and stared at the drone monitor.

"What the hell am I looking at?" asked Kit.

Chapman made a few adjustments to the monitor and now the images were a little larger and a lot clearer.

"That, my friend, is a whole lot of folks moving in single file from the desert to the edge of the north rim of the canyon."

"How many are there?"

"I think I count thirty-six. No, make it forty figures. They all appear to be armed. It looks like some kind of military operation."

"Are there any others or is that it?"

"Let me zoom out and have the drone do a wider pattern," said Chapman.

The drone responded and moved further east and slightly south of the position of the forty figures.

"Holy shit! There's more of them," said Chapman as he pointed at the monitor.

Sure enough, the monitor clearly showed ten more figures moving to a positon slightly south of the other group. While the drone held its pattern overhead, Chapman and Kit saw the ten figures move into a depression in the ground and take what looked like firing positons.

"What are those guys up to?" asked Kit.

"If I didn't know better, I'd say they were taking up a defensive positon," said Chapman.

"What would they be defending against?"

"I have no idea, but it certainly looks like either a defensive positon or some kind of ambush to me."

"I don't get whom they would be ambushing with all those other guys clear to the north of them," said Kit."

"Let's go back to the other group and see what's going on with them," said Chapman.

The drone responded to Chapman's changes to the joystick and flew quickly to the north.

"There they are," said Chapman. He slowed the speed on the drone and moved it to a spot above the group and held the drone in a hovering positon.

"The group is splitting up," said Chapman.

"Why would they do that?"

"I don't know, but, wait, they're setting up an ambush."

"An ambush?"

"About thirty of them are getting in position by creating a line extending east from the east edge of the canyon entrance. They are facing south. The other ten are linked with the others, but they form a line running north and south from the east end of the larger group of armed men."

"Why would they do that?" asked Kit.

"It's a classic L-shaped ambush, right out of the basic infantry tactics manual," said Chapman.

"Is it meant to be an ambush for us?"

"I don't think so. They would have no way of knowing if we would be coming out the canyon through the east entrance. Not to mention that we have never moved through the canyon at night."

"Then why are they doing it?"

"I can't be sure, but my guess is that they either think or they know that some Indians are coming through the canyon tonight."

"That would make sense if we were right about the Apaches. They could be coming back from Arizona with supplies for their camp someplace in the Sierra Madre Mountains."

"If the Apache have been making supply runs, chances are that the cartel has found out about it and has some idea of when they make their runs," said Chapman.

"So the cartel has finally arrived here in force. That can't be good for us or the Indians," said Kit.

"We're all right as long as they stay outside the canyon. I'm surprised they would come here at night."

"They've come here before at night when they were smuggling dope."

"The night does keep the Border Patrol from spotting them."

"I think it's time to give Swifty a call."

"I don't think strolling out through the canyon to pick a fight with about fifty cartel men sounds like such a good idea, Kit."

"I have no intention of picking a fight, but there is no guarantee that those cartel boys are going to just sit there all night. What if they decide to move into the canyon and start looking for our camp?"

"So what do you have in mind?"

"The east entrance to the canyon is pretty narrow about four hundred yards to the west of the entrance."

"So how does that help us?"

"It's a great place for us to set up our own ambush, and a great spot for me to provide oversight protection."

"Sounds like a plan. What should I do with the drone?"

"Keep the drone up and have it do a pattern over both positions of the cartel men. That way we'll know if they start to move into the canyon."

"Will do, Kit."

Kit pulled his satellite phone out of his vest and after acquiring a signal, he called Swifty.

"Swiflty here."

"Are you boys ready to go?"

"That's a stupid question. All of us here were born ready."

"We've got two groups of cartel boys setting up ambushes outside the east end of the canyon.

"Ambushes for us?"

"I don't think so. Chapman and I think it might be for the Apaches, but we're only guessing."

"Where do you want us to go?"

"You remember that spot where the canyon narrows about four hundred yards before you get to the east entrance?"

"Yeah, I do. It's narrow and has lots of rocks around it."

"That's the place. I want you four to move there and set up an ambush for the cartel boys."

"The cartel boys?"

"Right now they are setting in an ambush positon, but what if they change their minds and come into the canyon looking for us?"

"An ambush for the cartel, it is, Kit."

"Be sure and take all the ammo you can carry."

"We can do that, but why?"

"Chapman and I counted about fifty cartel boys out there."

"Fifty! Holy crap."

"They may not come, but I think we need to be ready. You have good weapons and you have night vision goggles, plus you have me up here providing oversight protection. We also have the drone to tell us where they're moving."

"I'll tell the others and we'll be moving in five minutes. Swifty out."

Jose walked carefully along the line of his men in their L-shaped ambush. All of them had found good cover behind bushes and rocks. Most, but not all of them had good fields of fire. Jose cursed his fate at having so many young thugs in his force. They were good for threatening, torturing, and killing simple peasants. He wondered how good they would be when they faced an enemy that was shooting back at them.

Jose was sure they would be facing the dreaded Bronco Apaches. If they were lucky they would catch the Apaches by surprise, but he felt in his gut it was unlikely they would be able to surprise the Apaches. He knew the history of his people with the Apaches. It was a history of mistrust, betrayal, and violence. He was not sure why the cartel bosses wanted an end to the Bronco Apaches, but he had a suspicion.

He had heard rumors the Bronco Apaches had established rancherias in the Sierra Madre and had managed to cultivate marijuana farms. The Apaches supposedly smuggled the marijuana into Arizona and used it to trade for supplies, which they transported back to their rancherias. The cartel did not allow any competition and their methods were brutal. Jose was pretty sure that was the real reason he was here with fifty armed men on a dark night.

Jose thought of vicious methods employed by the Apaches on their captives and found himself shivering, and it was not from the cold night wind.

Chapman had seen little movement from the cartel men after they had gone into their ambush positions.

He could see one figure moving along the line of the ambush and decided it must be the leader of the operation checking on the readiness of the ambush.

Kit nudged Chapman in the ribs.

"Maybe we should have another look-see at the trail coming down from the north rim?"

Chapman made adjustments on the computer and moved the joy-stick. The drone changed course and altitude and headed up to the north rim of Skeleton Canyon.

When Chapman had the drone about three hundred feet above the canyon rim, he leveled it off and had it begin a slow zig-zag pattern over the known location of the trail leading to the canyon rim.

The monitor revealing nothing that was emitting heat. After ten minutes, Chapman turned to Kit.

"Should we take a look at our boys and see where they are?" he asked.

"That sounds like a good idea to me," said Kit.

Chapman punched in new directions and used the joy-stick to move the drone over the canyon floor. Within a few minutes, he found four shapes moving rapidly to the east in the canyon.

"There they are," said Chapman.

"They're about ten minutes from the narrow part of the canyon."

Kit pulled the phone out of his vest and after obtaining a signal he called Swifty.

"Swifty here."

"Get the lead out of your ass. You should be in positon by now," yelled Kit.

"You think it's so easy to move in this canyon in the dark, even with night vision goggles, you try it."

"Let me know when you get into positon," said Kit.

"Will do, now quit bothering the hired help," said Swifty.

Kit laughed into the phone and said, "Kit out."

After replacing the phone in his vest, Kit turned on his night vision goggles and pulled them down over his eyes. He then selected a good spot on the canyon rim. He picked up his AR-10 and set the adjustable bi-pods to the correct height. He reached into his vest and pulled out a Magpul thirty round magazine and inserted it into his rifle. He turned on the EO-Tech holographic sight and set it to a brightness that gave him a good sight pattern.

Then he took off his cowboy hat and lowered himself into a prone positon, allowing him a great field of fire for all of the approaches to the east entrance of Skeleton Canyon. He was ready.

Chapman kept a close watch on the drone monitor and pulled his AK-47 close to his side and within easy reach. He directed the drone to do a search pattern over the two cartel positons. The drone responded and soon Chapman was watching for any change in the cartel men's positon.

Kit's phone buzzed and he rolled to his side to pull it out of his vest.

"Kit here."

"Gringos are in positon. Let the party begin."

"Roger that, gringo. No movement by the opposition."

"Screw them. Let 'em come. We're ready. Swifty out."

Kit hung up his phone, but left it on the ground next to him so he could grab it quickly if he needed it.

Swifty had placed Thor and Big Dave up in the rocks on the north side of the canyon and he and Chance on the south side. All four of them had good cover and excellent fields of fire. All of them had their night vision goggles on and their rifles at the ready.

A half hour passed and there was no movement from the cartel men at the east end of the canyon. Chapman decided to check out the trail on the north rim of the canyon again and the drone responded to his course and flight plan changes.

Within five minutes, the drone was in positon over the trail on the north rim. Chapman programed a zig-zag flight plan for the drone and the drone immediately responded. At a height of three hundred feet the drone speed slowed and Chapman had the drone follow the known trail from the edge of the canyon rim back to the northwest.

The drone was about half way through its flight plan when heat emitting images appeared on the drone monitor.

"Holy shit," said Chapman.

"What is it?" asked Kit.

"I've got several bogies on the north rim. They're about a hundred yards from the rim and heading toward it."

"How many bogies?"

"I think I see them all, now. There appear to be ten or twelve. They're moving through the rocks, so the images come and go as their heat images are shielded by the rocks."

"Are they armed?"

"I think so, but all of them are carrying what looks like heavy packs of some kind."

Kit grabbed his phone, pushed a button and waited for a signal. As soon as he had a tone, he called Swifty.

"Swifty here."

"Chapman has twelve bogies armed and carrying packs up on the north rim trail headed for the canyon."

"Apaches?"

"We think so. Does the trail come down to the canyon floor behind or in front of your position?

"The trail comes down right in front of our positon," said Swifty.

"We have to warn the Indians about the ambush without letting the cartel men know, so we don't end up with a giant massacre."

"Just how do you propose we do that? I ain't in favor of walking up to some armed Bronco Apaches in the dark and sayin' howdy. Sorry to bother you, but there's a whole passel of angry Mexicans waiting for you just outside the canyon."

"I've got an idea, you boys stay put. I'll get back to you."

"We ain't got no plans to hike into Mexico, so we'll be right here. Swifty out."

Kit hit the end button on the phone and slipped it back into his vest. He rose from the ground and slid next to Chapman.

"Anything new?"

"The twelve of them reached the rim and are starting down the trail into the canyon."

CHAPTER TWENTY-EIGHT

KIT TOOK THE NIGHT VISION binoculars from Chapman, and he focused them on where he thought the trail cut into the canyon wall. He quickly found the trail and after sweeping the binoculars up and down the trail, he quickly found the twelve heat emitting images. They were moving slowly down the trail. He could see all of them carried large packs on their backs.

"So what do we do now, Kit?"

"We need to find a way to warn the Indians they're walking into a trap, and we need to do it in a way the Mexicans can't hear or see."

"I don't know how we do that. We have no way to contact them. We don't exactly have their cell phone numbers. Maybe we could send smoke signals?"

"Actually all we need to do is somehow scare them," said Kit. He remembered a time back in Wyoming when he had used fire arrows to scare Mexican grave robbers from an Indian burial ground. This time he was fresh out of fire arrows.

"I've got an idea!"

"I'm all ears. What's your idea, Kit?"

"What if we were to use the drone to scare them?"

"How the hell would we do that? The drone has no weapons, no lights, and no ability to make noise."

"Can you dive bomb them with the drone?"

"What the hell do you mean, dive bomb them? It's a drone not a dive bomber."

"I mean can we have the drone come in low and fast right over their heads? Something like that in the dark ought to scare anyone."

Chapman sat back and thought for a moment.

"It's possible, but I can't be sure how accurate I can be doing that just by using the monitor. I could hit one of the Indians, or I could crash the drone. But, if I could do it and get close, the noise from the drone's rotors and the motion in the darkness would probably even scare me."

"I can't risk firing a warning shot. That would alert the Mexicans. I think this is our only chance. Get the drone in positon, and I'll call Swifty and let him know what we're doing."

"I'm on it," said Chapman.

Kit pulled out the phone and called Swifty.

"Swifty here."

"The Apaches are coming down the trail. We're going to use the drone to buzz them and try to scare them into retreating back up the trail."

"You're going to scare Apaches with a drone?"

"If you were out sneaking around in the dark and you got buzzed by a drone you couldn't see, wouldn't it scare you?"

"I'd at least go flat on my belly until I figured out what was going on," said Swifty. "Your plan is so stupid, it just might work. We'll be ready. Thanks for the update. Swifty out."

Chapman took the drone off auto-pilot and used the joy-stick and the monitor to fly the drone over the positons of the two cartel groups.

"There is no movement by the Mexicans, Kit."

"Let's give buzzing the Apaches a shot," said Kit.

Chapman piloted the drone back inside the canyon and he quickly located the Indians, who were almost down to the canyon floor.

Chapman had the drone circle over the Apaches. The lead Apache had reached the canyon floor.

"It's now or never," said Chapman and he brought the drone down in a steep dive towards the Apaches.

The drone had increased speed, and the result was even more noise from the four rotors. Chapman had the drone diving from the west and when it was about fifteen feet above the Indians, he brought it out of its dive. The drone leveled out only about three feet above the Apaches, and the result was about what Swifty had predicted.

The twelve Apaches immediately dove down and flattened out against the floor of the canyon. What happened next was not what Kit had anticipated.

Kit was watching the Indians when the drone buzzed them, and he was pleased that the drone did not hit any of them nor did it crash. Almost as soon as the Apaches hit the ground for cover, they rose up and dashed forward for the east entrance of the canyon, not back up the trail as Kit had hoped."

Kit's phone rang. It was Swifty.

"Great plan, genius. What do we do now?"

"Prepare to engage the Mexicans."

"Swifty out."

"I can't just let them run into an ambush," said Kit.

"They've stopped running and have hunkered down in some rocks," said Chapman who now had the drone back up over the canyon and was observing the Indians movements.

"Sooner or later they're going to continue moving out the east entrance," said Kit.

"I'm fresh out of ideas," said Chapman.

"Maybe it's time to let those Mexicans know Skeleton Canyon isn't a healthy place for them," said Kit.

"What do you mean, Kit?"

"As I recall, Mexicans are none too fond of fire arrows shot at them in the dark of night."

"Fire arrows?"

Before Kit could answer Chapman, Kit remembered using fire arrows to scare the Mexican grave robbers, and it triggered another idea.

Kit searched the pockets in his tactical vest that held ammo magazines for his rifle. Finally he found the magazine he was looking for. He took out the standard ammo magazine in his AR-10 and replaced it with the new magazine.

Kit had already put aside the binoculars and now assumed a prone positon with his night vision goggles on. He snapped the 3X magnifying scope on the rail so it was in front of the holographic sight and was quickly sighting in his AR-10 rifle.

The goggles gave him the images of the Mexicans lying on the ground in their ambush. He could see one Mexican standing upright about ten yards behind the ambush line. Unless Kit was mistaken, that had to be the leader of the cartel force.

Kit remembered what Big Dave had told him about combat. "Take out their leaders, and the rest of them will quickly lose interest."

Kit carefully brought the red dot in a red circle in his scope directly on the chest of the standing Mexican. It was a pretty long shot, and it was at a downward angle, but the AR-10 fired a 168 grain match point .308 tracer round that fired fast and flat.

Jose was cold, tired, and pissed. This was a wasted trip. He and his men had seen no Indians or gringos. He could already hear his men talking and had caught two of them smoking in violation of his orders to maintain secrecy.

Jose was thinking of his warm bed back in Mexico. He never heard the sound of a shot being fired until the slug hit him in the right shoulder. The impact knocked him to the ground.

The sound of the shot fired echoed through the canyon. The sight of their leader lying on the ground bleeding from his upper torso was too much for the cartel men. They, too had heard the rumors about the Bronco Apaches, and they had been uncomfortable lying on the desert floor in the dark for several hours. The dark had worked on their imaginations. They were not seasoned soldiers. They were thugs and rabble. They were the kind of predators who enjoy beating and killing helpless peasants. This was a different story. Death from the night was not something they were ready for.

Kit now began to fire tracer rounds just over the heads of the prone Mexicans. The sight of the red tracer rounds in the night sky was both awesome and terrifying to the Mexicans.

Kit saw several of the Mexicans jump to their feet and begin to flee back into the desert. The rest of the cartel men in the L-shaped ambush soon joined their comrades, as they began to run back to Mexico as fast as they could.

Kit decided to help them along. The AR-10 is a semi-automatic rifle with a thirty round magazine. He aimed his rifle just behind the fleeing men and began to pull the trigger. His put fifteen more tracer rounds down range, and the result was even more fear and confusion among the fleeing Mexicans.

In their confusion, the Mexicans had forgotten about Diaz and his nine men positioned in an arroyo. In the dark, Diaz had no idea who was in front of his position. He ordered his men to fire, and they did. The fire was wild and inaccurate and the result was a few of the fleeing Mexicans fired back at their unwitting comrades.

Within minutes, Diaz's frightened men had joined the others in a mad dash to Mexico.

Meanwhile, all of these events had unfolded in front of the twelve Apaches, who were gathered in the rocks at the base of the north rim of the canyon.

After a short time, the Apaches had regrouped and had decided to retreat back up the trail to the rim of the canyon, until they could sort out what awaited them beyond the east entrance to the canyon.

The Apaches had taken only a few steps in the darkness, when they were brought to a stop.

"Halt. Don't move. Drop your weapons. Do as you're told and you won't be harmed," yelled Swifty.

The Apaches appeared to be unsure as what to do when Big Dave managed to convince them to do as Swifty had ordered.

Big Dave fired an entire twenty round magazine from his BAR over the heads of the Apaches. The noise was deafening. It shocked the Apaches, and they reluctantly laid down their weapons.

Swifty stepped forward, looking like some giant alien bug with his dark clothing and night vision goggles over his eyes. He held his M-4 in a ready positon that gave no doubt he would use it if necessary. The other three men remained back in the darkness, so the Apache could not determine how few they really were.

"Do any of you speak English?" asked Swifty.

The Apaches looked at each other and finally one of them spoke.

"I speak English," said the Apache.

"Tell the rest of your friends to sit on the ground, away from their weapons."

"I don't think that'll be necessary," said the Apache.

"Why not?" asked Swifty.

"Because all of us speak English," replied the Apache.

"What's your name?" asked Swifty.

"My name is Kieta. I am Apache."

Swifty looked carefully at Kieta. He was about five foot ten inches in height with broad shoulders, long black hair and brown skin. He had a piece of cloth tied around his hair like a headband. He wore a long, loose fitting shirt that went down below his waist. He had on loose pants that were tucked into moccasin like boots that looked like leggings. Kieta was dressed like the Apaches Swifty had seen in pictures taken of Geronimo and his band of Chiricahua Apache back in 1886. The rest of the eleven Apaches were dressed in a similar fashion.

Kieta turned and motioned to the rest of the Apaches and they all became seated on the canyon floor. Kieta remained standing.

Swifty removed his night vision goggles.

"Those are nice NVGs," said Kieta.

"They look better than the ones I used in the Marines."

"You were in the Marines?" asked Swifty.

"I served as a Lance Corporal in the Marine Corps for five years," replied Kieta. I haven't seen tracer rounds at night in over ten years. I don't think those Mexicans have ever seen tracers before."

"I don't understand?" said Swifty.

"I was raised in Ft. Sill, Oklahoma, as part of the Chiricahua tribe located there after my people were released from prison in Florida. I enlisted in the Marines and after I got out, I came to Arizona."

"Why did you come to Arizona, and how did you end up like this?"

"In 1986 the state of Arizona lifted its ban on my people and since then some of the Chiricahua people have returned home. Most of them have joined other tribes because there were no Chiricahua in Arizona anymore. I joined the Mescalero tribe. I grew tired of reservation life, and heard stories of the Bronco Apaches living in Mexico. I came south looking for them and soon became one of them. The same is true for many of the others you see here."

"So you live in Mexico?"

"We have several rancherias in the Sierra Madre Mountains. They have been there since Massai began the first Bronco Apaches in 1888.

"How do you survive in a place like this?"

"We survive like our fathers and our fathers' fathers. We understand the land. It is our country and has been for hundreds of years. I know that might be hard for you to understand."

"I still don't get how you survive here. What are you doing coming down into this canyon from Arizona and heading to Mexico?"

"We grow and harvest a certain kind of crop in the mountains, and we bring the crop to Arizona to trade for supplies, which we take back to our rancherias."

"What kind of crop is this?"

"It's probably better you don't know," answered Kieta with a slight smile.

"You're probably right."

"So, exactly who are you and your men and what are you doing in Skeleton Canyon?" asked Kieta.

Swifty paused before answering. He could hear the sounds of footsteps and hooves on the canyon floor.

Kit and Chapman appeared out of the darkness leading the heavily loaded llama. Seated awkwardly on a smaller pack on the llama was a wounded Mexican. His hands were tied in front of him and his right shoulder was bandaged.

Swifty noted Kit was carrying his AR-10 at the ready positon.

"Kit, Chapman, good to see you. Come over here and join the party," said Swifty.

Kit walked up next to Swifty. "What've we got here, Swifty?"

"Kit, I'd like to introduce you to Kieta, a Chiricahua Apache. Kieta, this here is my best friend, Kit Andrews."

Kit instinctively put out his right hand and Kieta took it in a firm handshake.

"So what's going on, Swifty?"

"Kieta here and his friends are taking supplies back to their rancherias in the Sierra Madre Mountains in Mexico."

"I see," said Kit.

"Kieta and his men all speak English, Kit."

"They do?" said a surprised Kit.

"Kieta served as a Lance Corporal in the Marines for five years. He's originally from Oklahoma."

"Ft. Sill, Oklahoma?" asked Kit.

"That's right," answered Kieta.

"Kieta was just asking me who we are and what we're doing in Skeleton Canyon, Kit."

"That's a good question," said Kit.

Kit turned to look straight at Kieta. He noticed the man's eyes were dark as night, but he saw no fear in them.

"We're cowboys from Wyoming. We're not military or law enforcement or Border Patrol. We're just American citizens."

"You appear to be well-armed citizens," said Kieta.

"We're law abiding citizens, but we are always prepared to defend ourselves," replied Kit.

"Why did you fire on the Mexicans?"

"They'd set up an ambush for you and we tried to warn you with the drone."

"Drone?"

"A small remote controlled aircraft with a camera on it. We tried to scare you into returning back up the trail, and we failed. When that happened, we had no choice, but to try to run off the Mexicans."

"I assume he was one of the ambushers," said Kieta as he pointed to the wounded Mexican on the llama. His voice had become hard as he spoke.

"I needed to put the leader of the cartel boys down to be able to panic the rest of them."

"Why would you be concerned with protecting us?" asked Kieta.

"We ain't real friendly with the cartel, if you know what I mean. Once we figured out they had set up an ambush for you, we had to find a way to stop it."

"But why put yourself in danger to help us?"

"We've been trying to locate your people."

"Why? How did you know we even existed?"

"We came to Skeleton Canyon on a mission at the request of a friend."

"What kind of a mission?" asked Kieta.

"A brother of a friend of ours came into Skeleton Canyon. He was a teacher, who used his vacations to search for treasure. He disappeared, and local law enforcement had no luck finding him or what happened to him, so we came looking for him."

"When was this man in the canyon?" asked Kieta.

"A few months ago. No one saw or heard from him after he entered the canyon."

"That's not exactly correct," said Kieta.

"What do you mean?" asked Kit.

"This man you speak of. Did he have a name?"

"His name was Leon Turner. He was a white man."

"We saw your Mr. Turner."

"You saw him! Where did you see him?"

"We saw him enter the canyon. We were resting on the canyon rim. He was trying to climb a game trail on the south canyon wall. He slipped and fell about three hundred feet to the rocks below. We watched and waited for others to come to help him, but no one came. We came down the trail and went to find him. He was badly broken up in the rocks. He was still breathing when we reached him. We gave him some water, but he died about ten minutes later. We searched his body and found his wallet and driver's license. That's how we knew his name."

"What happened then?" asked Kit.

"We buried him in a small depression in the canyon. We covered his body with rocks to keep the coyotes from the body."

"Can you take me to where you buried him?" asked Kit.

"I can take you there and point it out to you, but we Apache consider the area around the dead to be bad medicine, so I can't take you to the exact site."

"It'll be dawn in an hour," said Swifty.

"We've spent a lot of time in this canyon. Another hour or so won't kill us," said Kit.

Big Dave had started a small campfire, which warded off the night chill and gave off a flickering light to the strange group surrounding it. The light flickered off the faces of Wyoming cowboys and Chiricahua Apaches. It was a very unlikely sight.

As soon as it was light, Kieta led Kit and Swifty to a spot near the bottom of the south rim of Skeleton Canyon. Kieta pointed to a cairn of rocks about forty yards away. Kit walked over to the cairn and he and Swifty began to remove the rocks in the cairn. After about ten minutes they had removed enough rocks to uncover a decomposing body of a white man.

Kit and Swifty both looked at the body for a few seconds and then looked at each other. Neither man knew what to do or say. After a brief pause, Kit took out his phone and took pictures of the body. Then he and Swifty replaced the rocks over the grave. Kit took out his GPS and marked the site as a waypoint on the unit. He took out his cell phone and took several pictures of the grave and the canyon wall behind it. Then he joined Kieta and Swifty, and they returned to the waiting cowboys and Apaches.

"What are you going to do with the Mexican?" asked Kieta as he pointed to the wounded Jose, who was now seated on the canyon floor.

"Well, we're going to wait until you and your men are long gone out of Skelton Canyon, and then we're going to call the Border Patrol. I'm pretty sure this Mexican is on one of their wanted lists," said Kit.

"What about the evidence of what happened here last night?" asked Kieta. "Won't the Border Patrol be suspicious."

"What evidence?" asked Big Dave. He held out a small webbed sack that held all the brass from the magazine he had fired from his BAR. Kit held out a similar bag full of .308 brass from his AR-10.

Kieta smiled.

"So we are free to go?" Kieta asked.

"Far as we're concerned, you were never here, Kieta," said Kit.

Kieta looked at the six cowboys from Wyoming. "I appreciate what you men did for us. If ever you are in this country again and you have need of help, you can count on us."

Kit held out his hand, and Kieta took it in a firm handshake.

"My people have an ancient custom. When men become friends, they often celebrate that friendship with an exchange of gifts," said Kieta.

"What kind of gift did you have in mind?" asked Kit.

"I'd really like to have one of those night vision goggles you have. It would really come in handy," said Kieta.

Kit slipped the goggles off his head and handed them to Kieta. Kieta took them and slipped them into his pack. When he removed his hand from his pack, he held an object. He placed the object in Kit's hand.

Kieta turned and headed for the east entrance of Skeleton Canyon, and the rest of the Apaches followed.

Kit looked down at the object in his hand. It was an Apache tomahawk.

When Kit looked up again, the Apaches were gone.

CHAPTER TWENTY-NINE

THE SIX MEN HEADED BACK to their camp in Pine Canyon. Swifty led the group, and Chapman brought up the rear with the llama and the Mexican.

Big Dave and Thor cooked up a huge breakfast of bacon, eggs, flapjacks, and biscuits. All of this was washed down with lots of hot coffee. After breakfast, the men packed up all their gear and loaded the animals in the horse trailers.

Kit gave Buck Slaughter a call and arranged for him to meet them at the gate in an hour. The caravan of three trucks and trailers slowly pulled out of Pine Canyon and began the slow trek through the narrow confines of Skeleton Canyon. When the trucks reached the ranch stock tank, they stopped to unload and water the mules and llamas.

"What are you planning to do with the Mexican?" asked Swifty.

"I'm planning to hand him over to Buck. He's guilty of trespassing, and I think Buck will be happy to hand him over to the Border Patrol."

"I hope so," said Swifty. "Buck didn't seem none too fond of Mexicans."

Kit was about to answer Swifty when his words were drowned out by the noise of an approaching Border Patrol helicopter. Both men held onto their hats as the copter landed in an open area next to the stock tank.

The copter landed and the passenger door slid open and out stepped Captain Vonalt. He jogged over to where Kit and Swifty were standing.

"Surely you boys weren't going to leave without saying good-bye", said the smiling Vonalt.

"We was just about to give you a call," said Swifty.

"I'll bet you were," said the captain. "Well, here I am, saving you the trouble. Did you find your missing man?"

"We did, Captain. We found his grave."

"I'm not surprised, but I'm glad you found him. Where was the grave?"

Kit showed the captain the coordinates on his GPS along with the pictures he had taken. The captain took out a notebook and wrote down the coordinates and Kit's name and the date.

"When you get to Bisbee, stop and see the coroner and show him your information and your pictures. I'll let him know you're coming and he can take care of recovering the body."

"Will do, Captain," said Kit.

The captain pointed over to the wounded Mexican, who was setting on the ground by the stock tank. "Just who might that unfortunate fellow be?"

"He's a cartel member we happened to run into and when he didn't want to come along peaceable like, we shot him," said Kit.

"As ridiculous as that sounds, I'm inclined to believe you, Kit."

"We patched him up. I'm pretty sure he's on your list of bad guys," said Kit.

Captain Vonalt walked over to where the Mexican sat. He got down on one knee and looked him in the face.

"Well, well, if it isn't our old friend Jose Escobar."

"You know him?" asked Kit.

"Jose is late of the Mexican Army, where he deserted after stealing government funds. Since then, he's been reportedly working for the cartel."

"So he's one of the bad guys," said Kit.

"Yes, he is. You know, I don't' think Jose is glad to see me. Can you imagine that?" said Captain Vonalt.

Vonalt motioned to one of his men who untied Jose's hands and replaced the rope with steel handcuffs. Then the agent led Jose to the waiting helicopter. Captain Vonalt followed, pausing before getting back in the copter to touch the brim of his hat to Kit and Swifty in a one handed salute."

The helicopter lifted off and after the copter and its accompanying noise disappeared into the desert sky, quiet returned to the area around the stock tank.

After having been watered, the mules and llamas were loaded back into the trailers, and the convoy of three trucks headed for the gate to the ranch.

When they reached the gate, Buck was waiting for them.

"Hey there, Kit, Swifty. Good to see you boys again. How did it go? Did you find that lost guy?"

Kit got out of his truck and shook Buck's hand.

"It went really well. We did find the location of the body."

"I kind of figured he had to be dead after all this time, especially in that damned canyon."

"He died of a fall the first day he was in the canyon. He was buried under a cairn of rocks by the south wall of the canyon."

"How the hell did you find the grave?"

"We had a little help," said Kit.

"Help from whom?"

"Let's just say we got some help from the ghosts of Skeleton Canyon," said Kit with a smile.

Buck just shook his head and grinned back. He opened the gate, and the three truck convoy passed through and headed north on Highway 80.

They drove to Bisbee and stopped at the same motel where they had stayed before. After checking in they went to the same Mexican Restaurant and ate a huge lunch and got roaring drunk on a large number of pitchers of Coors beer accompanied by the occasional shot of good bourbon.

The next morning Kit pulled himself out of bed, nursing a raging hangover. He showered and dressed and went straight to an ice cream shop, where he drank down a huge chocolate milkshake. He had learned from his younger days in Chicago that a milkshake does wonders by lining the stomach and making a hangover feel much better.

After taking three aspirin with a Coke, he made his way over to the coroner's office. There he met with the coroner, who had been expecting him. Kit explained he had found the grave of the missing Leon Turner. He gave the coroner the exact location of the grave by longitude and latitude from his GPS waypoint. Then he forwarded the pictures of the body and the grave from his cell phone to the coroner's e-mail. After giving the coroner his personal information so he could be reached for any further questions, Kit walked over to the plaza.

There he sat on a bench in the shade of an old cottonwood tree and pulled out his cell-phone.

"Hello, is this the nurse emergency call service?"

"If you get any emergency service from me, it will be dang expensive, Cowboy."

"I just wanted you to know that we found Leon."

"Oh, my God! What happened to him?"

"It seems he fell off a game trail on the south wall of the canyon on his first day in the canyon. He died shortly after he fell from his injuries. We found him buried under a cairn of rocks. I've given the information to the Cochise County Coroner in Bisbee. They'll be heading out there today to recover the body. You can tell Leslie the news and tell her to contact the coroner, and they'll help with the arrangements on getting his body home."

"I was afraid he was dead. I'm not looking forward to telling Leslie what happened."

"I'm glad it's you telling her and not me," said Kit.

"Thank you, Kit. I can't tell you how much I appreciate you helping out my friend. I just knew you'd be the one to help her and the one to find out what happened to Leon. I'm sorry to put you to all this trouble. I felt badly about asking for your help. I didn't want you to think I was taking advantage of you, but there was no one else I could think of that might be able to help Leslie.

"I'm happy I could help," said Kit. "I was glad to be able to do something for you. I can never repay you for what you did for me in the Wind River Mountains."

"I just did what I was trained to do, but I will admit I'm glad I was there. When I reached down to check your wound, I felt something electric and I guarantee you it wasn't the sight of blood."

"I thought I was in heaven and I was looking at an angel," said Kit.

"I miss you. When can you come to Boulder?"

"I miss you too, Shirley. It'll take us a while to get back to Wyoming. As soon as I get home, I'll give you a call and let you know when I'm coming."

"Great. I'll look forward to your call."

"Shirley, there's one more thing."

"What's that?"

"We can also talk about you coming to Wyoming for a visit."

"I'd like that, Cowboy."

"So would I."

"Oh, Kit."

"Yes."

"Just how did you manage to find out where Leon was buried?"

Kit paused before answering. "I'll tell you all about it when I see you in Boulder. For now, let's just say I got some help from the ghosts of Skeleton Canyon."

"You are a very strange and mysterious man, Kit Andrews."

"Don't I know it," said Kit, and he hung up the phone.

It took Kit and his friends two days to get back to Wyoming. After dropping Swifty off, Kit pulled into the front of his father's house in the hills outside Kemmerer.

Kit had no sooner alighted from his truck when his father came out the side door of the house.

Kit braced himself for what he expected to be a barrage of questions about the trip to Skeleton Canyon. Instead, he got a surprise.

"Kit, I know you're tired, but I've got something I need to show you," said his dad.

The next thing Kit knew he was sitting in the passenger seat of his father's pickup truck and they were driving into Kemmerer.

Even though Kit had tried to get his dad to tell him what was going on, his father had refused to give him a hint of what they were going to see.

Finally his father pulled over and parked the truck in front of the old First National Bank building which was located across from the city park in the triangle that made up the center of town.

Both men got out of the truck and stepped up on the sidewalk.

"What's this all about?" asked Kit.

"I thought it was time you moved out of my house and got a place of your own, Kit."

"A place of my own? Why? Are you uncomfortable with me living in your house?"

"Hell no. I'm happy you're living in my house. It's just that I found a place that seemed perfect, and so I bought it for you."

"You bought it for me?"

"That's what I just said."

"Where is it?" asked Kit.

"Right in front of you," said his father.

Kit looked at his father in disbelief.

"The old bank building? This place has been empty for at least three years. You want me to live in a bank?"

"This old bank building is over a hundred years old. It's solid masonry and built like a brick shit house. The entire first floor contains two large vaults complete with steel vault doors. The second floor is a huge apartment. There's a working elevator, and the basement is perfect for an indoor pistol range. The drive-in can be walled in and it will make a four car garage with doors at each end. The alarm system still works."

"I bought it for you, but you have to finish it the way you want it and that comes out of your pocket. In the end you'll have a place to run your business and a place to live in the same location."

"What business? I don't have a business."

"I think you do. You've developed a business you're good at and one that definitely seems to fill a market niche. You just need to start getting paid for what you do."

"I've helped people who couldn't pay."

"No reason to stop doing that. Just collect from the ones who can pay."

"I still don't get it."

Kit's father went back to his truck and pulled a hand-lettered sign out of the truck bed. He carried it over to where Kit was standing and held it up for Kit to read.

The sign was painted green with white letters that spelled out the following:

ROCKY MOUNTAIN SEARCHERS
KEMMERER, WYOMING

"You're gonna need these," said Kit's father as he tossed him the keys to the building.

Kit used the keys to open the front door and followed as his father led him on the official tour of his new home.

THE END

ACKNOWLEDGEMENT

THIS NOVEL IS A WORK of fiction. There is no connection between any of the characters in this novel and any persons living or dead. I became interested in Skeleton Canyon while reading about Geronimo's surrender to General Nelson Miles in Skeleton Canyon in 1886.

Further research revealed the legend of the buried silver treasure in the canyon. While reading about the legend, I discovered the story of the Chiricahua Apache named Massai. Massai really did exist, and he did escape from the heavily guarded train taking the Chiricahua Apaches from Arizona to prison in Florida. He did return to Arizona after a one year long twelve hundred mile journey, and he is considered by some to be the founder of what became known as the Bronco Apaches.

My research led me to a book by journalist and historian Douglas V. Reed of El Paso, Texas. The book *They Never Surrendered* is a historical study of the Bronco Apaches of the Sierra Madres from 1890 to 1935.

My research included trips to St. Augustine, Florida, where I discovered the Spanish fort there served as a prison for the Chiricahua Apaches, and to Cochise County, Arizona. I had intended to hike into Skeleton Canyon but was stopped by the locked gate on Skeleton Canyon Road. The road has been closed by local ranchers since 2005 because of their disgust with local law enforcement for not dealing with the never ending traffic of illegals and drug smugglers through the canyon and trespassing over their ranch property.

I wish to thank my long-time friend Kerry Wong and my very patient wife Nancy L. Callis for proof reading my work and for offering more politically correct alternatives to my writing. I would also like to thank the readers who have contacted me with their thoughts and suggestions on my previous books. I enjoy the feed-back and encourage readers of this novel to contact me at rwcallis@aol.com with their thoughts.

This is the fourth novel in a series about some mythical people who exist only in my imagination. When I finished my first book *Kemmerer*, my older sister Cherrill Flynn called me and asked what was going to happen next to Big Dave and Kit. That's when I realized that I wasn't done telling stories and soon *Hanging Rock* was created, followed by *Buckskin Crossing*.

I am currently sifting through some ideas for a fifth story about Big Dave, Kit, and Swifty.

I write because I enjoy it. The best reward for my work is to hear from readers about what they liked and didn't like in my books.

I hope you enjoyed reading *Ghosts of Skeleton Canyon* as much as I did writing it.

Robert W. Callis